North Ayrshire Libraries

**This book is to be returned on or before
the last date stamped below.**

2 9 MAR 2008   1 4 JAN 2010

- 9 MAY 2008   2 1 JAN 2010

1 5 MAY 2008 -5 MAR 2010

- 6 AUG 2007   1 7 MAY 2010

1 7 AUG 2007   2 9 JUL 2008

7 AUG 2007   - 3 JUL 2010   2 3 AUG 2010

- 4 SEP 2008

- 6 OCT 2008   - 3 9 SEP 2010   9 DEC 2010

2007   0 1 NOV 2008

2007

1 2 JAN 2009   1 4 FEB 2011

7 APR 2009   2 5 NOV 2011   1 7 FEB 2012

MAY 2009   - 8 JUN 2012

JUN 2009

NEWED BY TELEPHONE

Missing

Missing

CATH STAINCLIFFE

First published in Great Britain in 2007 by
Allison & Busby Limited
13 Charlotte Mews
London W1T 4EJ
www.allisonandbusby.com

Copyright © 2007 by CATH STAINCLIFFE

The moral right of the author has been asserted.

A CIP catalogue record for this book is available from
the British Library.

10 9 8 7 6 5 4 3 2 1

ISBN 0 7490 8025 6
978-0-7490-8025-9

Typeset in 11/16 pt Sabon by
Terry Shannon

Printed and bound in Wales by
Creative Print and Design, Ebbw Vale

CATH STAINCLIFFE is the author of six previous Sal Kilkenny novels, including *Looking for Trouble* which was shortlisted for the CWA John Creasey award. She is also a scriptwriter, the creator of ITV's *Blue Murder* starring Caroline Quentin. Based in Manchester, she is the mother of three children and a founder member of Murder Squad.

Acknowledgements

Thanks to Jane, Maggie, Mary and Pat –
a real pleasure as ever.

Dedication

With love to my new-found brothers and sisters:
Padraig, Sarah, Ian, Jim, Yvonne, Oonagh and Stan.

CHAPTER ONE

People disappear every day. Most of them choose to. Have you ever been tempted? Slip on a coat, pick up your bag and walk, or drive, or run. Turn your back on home, family, friends, work.

Why do people do it? Because they can? Because staying feels harder than leaving? Because they are angry or desolate or simply, deeply, mind-numbingly bored with the life they have? Because their heart is breaking and their mind fragmenting? And the grass is greener, the flowers smell sweeter. And if they stay they might be truly lost.

Back in June, the same week that I'd just found one person, two more went missing. None of them related. The only connection was me; Sal Kilkenny, my job; private investigator. And finding people seemed to be the flavour of the month.

I was about to ring Bob Swithinbank, to tell him I'd traced the birth mother who had relinquished him for adoption some thirty years ago, when the doorbell rang. I climbed upstairs from the basement office that I rent and opened the front door to my new client. 'You found it all right?'

'No problem.'

'Come in. We're downstairs.'

Trisha Marlowe was a striking-looking woman in her mid-thirties. She had straight, glossy, black hair cut short, the fringe spiky. A style that looked easy but probably needed daily attention with the mousse and the GHD straighteners. Her milky brown skin and deep brown eyes indicated mixed-race ancestry. I later learnt she was Anglo-Indian. She wore high quality casual clothes: black moleskin jeans, a cream fitted jacket and suede boots. I caught a scent of her perfume: light, grassy, not too overpowering.

A small sofa and easy chair were a recent addition to my office furniture. I tended to make snap judgements with new clients as to where to sit with them. Some seemed suited to the formality of desk and chairs, others to the more relaxed option. Without any cue from me, Trisha Marlowe picked the sofa.

'The reason I'm here,' she began, 'is that Janet, my friend, has gone missing. I'm worried about her. She's got children you see, and she'd never leave them.'

'Has she been gone long?'

'Nearly a week. Mark, that's her husband, he's been to the police, reported it but there doesn't seem to be very much they can do.'

Leaving home isn't a crime. The police would have added her details to the Missing From Home files but they wouldn't do more than that. Not unless there were suspicions of foul play linked to her disappearance.

'She's not done anything like this before?'

'No.'

'Anything difficult going on? Trouble in the marriage, depression, a new relationship?'

Trisha frowned and shook her head. 'No, I mean, I know

things were a bit rocky between her and Mark – they've had some bad luck recently. He lost his job and I think things have been tricky financially but nothing really serious. And anything else, anyone else – she'd have told me. We're really close.'

'How old are the children?'

'Five and eight. I'm their godmother. We don't know what to tell them.' She pressed her lips together, a sudden need to rein in her emotions. I sensed she was close to tears and waited.

'I'm really worried.' She tapped her knuckles under her chin, her hand moving to some rhythm of anxiety. She described how they had contacted local hospitals to make sure that Janet hadn't been involved in an accident, and that other friends and relatives had been alerted. 'No one's seen her or heard from her,' she said.

'Did she take anything with her? Passport, bags, jewellery?'

'No. Mark says her handbag's gone but that's all. We're not sure what she was wearing...' she faltered. 'You know what men are like – clothes.' She gave a small smile.

'And when did she go?'

'Thursday.'

Today was Wednesday; six nights away from her family, from her children.

I asked Trisha to tell me everything she could about that day. She explained that Janet was between jobs. She was a supply teacher and had been doing several weeks cover at a primary school in Stockport, a neighbouring town. The teacher she was replacing had returned from sick leave. Although money was tight for the family, Janet was glad to finish there. The school had been in a poor area and the children were very demanding. Many of them had special needs but the school hadn't been able to provide the extra staffing and resources the children required. Consequently, much of Janet's time was spent trying to exert discipline and retain control.

Trisha had spoken to Janet on the Wednesday night. Janet planned to spend Thursday pottering about and catching up on household chores. Mark was going to a job interview in Liverpool. He left early to avoid the rush hour. Janet walked the children to school. At four o'clock, the school secretary rang the house. No one had come to collect Isobel and Jacob. When there was no reply, the secretary rang the mobile numbers they had on file. Janet's was switched off, but Mark answered his. He was en route back to Manchester. He apologised for the apparent mix-up and drove straight to the school. He was there forty minutes later.

When there was still no sign of Janet by six o' clock, Mark began to feel uneasy. At seven, he rang Trisha. Then he tried other friends and family. At ten o' clock, he spoke to the police for the first time.

'Can you try and find her?' Trisha asked me.

'Yes. It could take time though, and I have had cases where I've not been able to trace someone. Some people – they just stay missing. It's incredibly difficult for the family, for everybody, but it does happen.'

'But a mother—' she protested.

'It happens.'

I fetched a contract from my files and asked her to read it.

'There will probably be a lot of waiting around,' I told her.

'Information tends to come in fits and starts. When I've done the equivalent of two days' work, we can review things. You can decide whether to carry on. The fees can soon mount up.'

'That's not a problem,' she waved her hands in dismissal. 'It's the least I can do. I feel so...useless. There's Mark and the children—' she shook her head.

'I'd like to start by talking to him.'

Trisha promised to arrange a time for the following day and gave me all the details I needed.

Once she'd left, I made myself a coffee and opened a file on Janet Florin. The name made me smile. Coins from the olden days. Was a florin the one with a wren on? I'd a few old pennies at home, Maddie liked to use them to play shop, the large copper discs, dark with age, almost filled her palm. Florin. Did having a particular name make any difference to a person? If your surname was Flowers or Peace did life run that bit smoother? Did the Bleakleys and the Paines tread a harder path?

When I'd finished my coffee, I took a moment to think through my next call. Then I dialled the number.

'Bob, it's Sal Kilkenny, I have some news. Are you sitting down?' I kept my voice light but it was a serious suggestion.

'Oh, God. Have you found her?' Bob Swithinbank's voice was high with emotion. I pictured him gripping the phone: a big man swathed in black leathers, with a balding head and a thin, brown ponytail, a beer belly and far too many facial piercings.

'Yes. We've got an address. It's actually in Manchester and Sandra is still living there according to the Electoral Records. I've sent the letter there.'

Acting as an intermediary, I had written a carefully worded letter which didn't say anything too obvious but would alert Sandra to the fact that Bob was hoping for some sort of contact. It referred to the month and year when she had him and the place and said that someone who had known her briefly then was hoping for news. I'd left my details and number for her to ring and wrote that I was hoping she would be in touch when she had taken some time to think things over.

'Oh, thank God.' His voice broke and then there were huffing and snuffling sounds.

And I sat there gripping the phone, and blinking back tears. Some days, work is like that. Telling people what they're longing to hear. And I love it.

CHAPTER TWO

I was dithering over cheeses on the dairy aisle, when I heard someone call my name. I turned to find Rachel, an old friend and notorious chatterbox, beaming at me. A young man was at her side; dark hair, slight build, his olive skin pitted and grainy.

'I was going to ring you tomorrow,' she said. 'You remember Ramin?'

I nodded, not that I remembered him well, but I recognised him as one of the asylum seekers that Rachel knew. She's a full-time social worker but outside office hours she'd become involved in a support group for Iranian asylum seekers in Manchester. They'd had a fund-raising event a few weeks before and Rachel had dragged all her friends along, myself included.

'I wanted to ask you a favour,' she said.

Rachel had helped me out more than once when I needed a social worker's input to a case. I owed her. 'Go on,' I said.

'Ramin's brother, Berfan, has gone missing. I'm swamped at work and my boss'll get sniffy if I start using the phone to check places out.' She grimaced. 'If you could ring round the hospitals? He's probably landed on his feet somewhere, got a bit of work perhaps.' The reassurance sounded hollow to me.

I think she was just trying to cheer Ramin up.

He smiled sadly. 'The paper,' he reminded her.

'Yeah. He got his refusal a couple of weeks ago,' Rachel told me. 'They want to send him back to Iran, deport him. So there is a chance he's gone underground.'

'He will tell me,' Ramin insisted.

'Maybe,' Rachel said. 'But maybe he thinks you are safer if you don't know.'

Ramin shrugged, glanced away, his jaw working.

'I'll do what I can,' I told him. 'A picture would be useful, a photo.'

'I have one,' he nodded.

'I can call round. Is tomorrow afternoon OK?' Daft question really, asylum seekers weren't allowed to work, they'd no money. The opportunities for a busy diary were somewhat limited.

They gave me an address in Longsight, not far from the street market, and Ramin's mobile number. If I heard anything before then I promised to let him know. He thanked me quietly.

Rachel asked me how we all were. Fine, I told her, but I needed to get back as our tea was in the trolley and the kids would be ravenous. I wanted to escape before Rachel had a chance to invite me for a get-together. Despite my assurances, all was not well at home. Everything was off-kilter. But I didn't want to tell her about it. Ray, my long-time housemate, and I had broken all our rules, unspoken and customary, and found ourselves in a clinch one night. I had been upset and confused by some terrible events at work and Ray had comforted me. But his brotherly concern had morphed into something much more passionate and I'd responded. Or my body had. Until I pulled away before things could go any further.

Since then, Ray had behaved like a lovesick teenager. To my mortification, he had dumped his steady girlfriend Laura and then he'd tried to woo me again. But I was still bewildered. I'd never really fancied Ray – oh, he's pretty enough, dark Italian colouring, attractive face (if you ignore the moustache), slim build – but I'd never thought of him in that way. Till now. And it was doing my head in.

The other aspect that puzzled me was why Ray had suddenly fallen for me. His interest had come out of the blue. My own lurch of desire could be explained by the trauma I'd been through – an urge to seize life after a frightening brush with death. But his?

Now we were living in a sort of limbo, taut with sexual tension and emotional strain. A couple of times, Ray had tried to talk to me about it but I'd put him off. We had to deal with it sometime; it was messing us up and threatening our future. There were the kids to think about too. Ray's son Tom and my daughter Maddie had grown up like brother and sister. If we couldn't sort out our relationship, it would jeopardise theirs and the home we all shared. I needed to face up to things and find time to discuss everything with Ray. The prospect simmered on the horizon like an electric storm.

I was dishing up the tea when Ray arrived home. I could feel his eyes on me. It was unnerving. Beforehand, I'd been part of the furniture – well, maybe more than that but not worth all this gazing and staring.

'Garlic bread?' I offered.

'Please.'

Now each piddling exchange was laden with significance. The whole thing was exhausting. I engaged the children in chatter about school as a means of diversion. After tea, I helped Maddie with her homework. Then I put both of them to bed. Read a couple of chapters of *The Wee Free Men*, a Pratchett story which forced me to adopt a terrible Scottish accent. I heard Ray going out – taking Digger for a walk.

It was a lovely evening, the sky a turquoise blue streaked with patches of cloud dyed purple and orange from the setting sun. The evening star was glittering, rising to meet the night.

Breathing in the scent from wallflowers and lilac, I took a turn round the back garden. It's a reasonable size, attached to the big Victorian semi we shared. The early clematis had faded, its flowers turned to teasels. The apple tree was in leaf, the blossom gone and the fruit beginning to set where the flowers had been. In the corner of the lawn where the patio ends I had marked out an irregular shape with a trail of sand from the kid's sandpit: the proposed site for my garden pond. It wasn't going to be that big, it was good to have lots of space for the kids to play, but it would make a nice home for some fish and frogs one day. The shape looked fine.

In the remaining hour of daylight, I dug out the hole, shovelling the loamy earth into the wheelbarrow and tipping it into the compost heap at the bottom of the garden. The heavy work soon had me sweating, it made my breath quicken

and my back ache and aggravated my sore shoulder. I drank
in the thick, rich scent of the soil, enjoyed the crisp noise of
the spade cutting through the turf and into the ground and the
tapestry of sounds, natural and urban, as I worked.
Chirruping birds settling for the night, the susurrus of traffic,
the rumble and roar of a plane, its light like a gliding star, and
the distant shrieks of giddy teenagers.

When I'd done, I sat on the bench on the patio for a while,
happily shattered, my boots laden with clods of soil.

Ray found me there.

'Busy?' His voice was warm, light.

'Digging the pond.' Obviously.

He sat beside me. I felt my skin tighten, my mouth dry. He
touched his hand to my chin.

'I'm muddy,' I managed. Ray was always more fastidious
than me.

'Are you?' He was very close. His eyes were black in the
twilight. I looked into them, then at his lips. Heat rippled
through me.

He kissed me.

I kissed him back.

Smooth lips, the unfamiliar springy feel of his moustache,
his hand on my back, my neck, in my hair. Everything
tingling, melting.

We kissed until I became dizzy and I pulled away with a
little moan.

'Sal.'

He wanted more and if I stayed there, he'd have got it. But
I wasn't ready. If this thing was going anywhere, it was going
there slowly.

I put my finger on his lips. 'Night.'

He caught my wrist, pressed his mouth to my palm. Then let me go. I walked away unsteadily, excitement trilling round my veins, bubbles of fear too. What on earth was I getting myself into?

CHAPTER THREE

Thursday was mapped out for me. Check with the hospitals first thing, to see if Berfan had been admitted, Mark Florin after that, Ramin in the afternoon then pick the kids up from school and an evening out with my best friend Diane.

There are loads of Accident and Emergency departments close to Manchester. We're a big city surrounded by others on all sides: Oldham, Salford, Stockport, Ashton. It took me forty minutes to verify that no one had admitted Berfan.

Janet and Mark Florin had a house in Stretford, handy for the football and the cricket at Old Trafford. Theirs was a three-bed semi-detached built in the ubiquitous Manchester red brick. The suburban street was fairly broad with a few cherry trees along the roadside but they did little to break up the stark uniformity of the rows of houses, each with its small front garden, driveway and garage. The flavour of the area was respectable, settled, dull. A place where people soaped their cars on Sunday mornings, joined the Neighbourhood Watch scheme, and got uneasy if a property sold to a developer who would rent it out.

There was a Rover parked outside which I recognised as Trisha Marlowe's, and a more modest Vauxhall Cavalier in the driveway. Small touches enhanced the look of the place:

conifers and grasses in the front garden and vigorous ivy, which covered much of the frontage. But the tub beside the front door and the manger on the lounge window sill had been neglected. The remnants of spring bulbs and winter bedding stood stiff and yellowing. It was a sunny day with a fresh wind and the stalks nodded and shivered in the breeze.

The bell gave a brittle shrill. Trisha answered the door. She greeted me warmly and took me into the front room where Mark was waiting. His son Jacob was sprawled on the floor playing on an Xbox, which was hooked up to a large entertainment centre, and arguing. 'But I haven't completed the level.'

'Just do it, Jacob.' Mark spoke sharply.

'But Dad...'

'Jacob...' Trisha tried.

'For Christ's sake, just do as you're damn well told.' Mark Florin erupted, his face purpling with rage.

The boy scrambled to his feet, pale with shock and ran from the room.

'Oh, God.' Mark pressed his fist against his mouth and nose, closed his eyes. 'Sorry,' he got to his feet. 'Just give me a minute.' He went after his son. I could hear him climbing the stairs.

Trisha raised her eyebrows. 'Jacob is off sick. We've all been walking on eggshells. I think he wants to stay close to home.'

It was understandable. The child must be bewildered; Mummy gone and everyone behaving oddly.

Trisha muted the volume on the TV.

There was a clump of tall grass outside the windows and I watched the sunlight cast flickering shadows onto the pale lemon walls. The longest wall was hung with lots of framed photographs: the children at various ages and stages, Janet and Mark sporting backpacks – student days, then on a beach and older now at a christening. The kids took after him, sturdy and dark. Janet was fairer, thinner. There were a couple of paintings on the other walls: landscapes that looked a little old-fashioned among the decor. It was a comfortable family room: two matching sofas in dark grey, a blue-grey flecked carpet, lemon curtains with a white stripe. Someone had carefully coordinated it all. The mid-range entertainment centre with DVD-RW and video had pride of place. Side tables sported a mish-mash of toys, magazines and papers.

Mark returned. He was a squat man with a bullish neck and his short, dark hair was receding. 'I said you'd go up,' he told Trisha.

'Fine.' She left us.

Mark sighed and turned to me. 'So you're the detective? And what can you do that the police can't?'

Rudely stated but a reasonable question.

'I can give some time to trying to trace your wife. The police can't.'

'Are you usually successful?'

'That varies.'

He grunted and sat down. He rubbed at his face with his hands. Big blocky hands. He had the build of a rugby player or a brickie. 'So, what do you want to know?' He sounded tired.

'A list of her contacts is essential. Everybody, not just friends and family but her optician, dentist, hairdresser, whatever. If she has an address book?'

He nodded.

'You can tell me who you've already spoken to. Any email contacts as well, clubs she belonged to. A recent photograph. What about her diary?'

'She's got her bag, it'd be in there.'

'Where do you think she's gone?'

'I haven't a clue,' he said wearily. 'It doesn't make sense. She didn't take anything with her, she didn't say anything. You know what I keep thinking?' He turned to me, his eyes glimmered. I expected him to say he thought Janet was dead. 'It's like the *Marie Celeste*. It's like that.' He waved his hands like a conjuror. 'Vanished.'

'Beforehand – how was she? Was anything different?'

'No.' His hand flew to his lips as he spoke. Was he lying?

'It might not seem significant to you but anything you can remember?'

'There was nothing.'

'Trisha said you had some financial difficulties.'

'Yes, we do. You try paying a mortgage and bringing up two kids on one salary.'

'Did you argue about money?'

'What are you getting at?' His neck flushed crimson, he scowled. He stood up. 'It wasn't my idea, getting someone like you, and I can do without you poking your nose in. Janet didn't leave because of any of that, we were fine.' He was hardly convincing.

'Really?' I didn't disguise my scepticism.

He met my eyes, contempt in his own. Then he looked away. He sat back down and studied the floor as he spoke. 'I think she might have been seeing someone.'

'Why?'

'Nothing obvious. Just she seemed happier, had more...more energy. Nothing had changed. I'd still got nothing and she hated the Stockport job. It was just a feeling. I could be wrong.'

'Any idea who it could have been?'

'None.'

'Did you ask her?'

'No.'

'Did you mention this to the police?'

'I couldn't – it's only a hunch. I was probably imagining it.'

'And the only thing you noticed was her mood?'

'Yes.' He rubbed at his face again, cleared his throat. 'No,' he amended. He coughed and shuffled, rubbed at the back of his neck. 'She was more interested in sex.'

His directness took me by surprise.

'We'd been tired, busy; the kids and everything. We no longer...it didn't happen very often. She seemed keen again.' His face was burning red. 'I'll get that address book.'

While he escaped to fetch things, I weighed up what I'd learnt and what else I needed.

'Ask the phone company for a bill,' I told him when he came back in. 'All the calls will be itemised and that might help us. And find any recent bank or credit card statements of hers.'

'Right, I'll have a look.' He passed me a handwritten list, names of people ticked off. 'These are the ones we got in touch with. Nobody's heard from her. They all promised to let me know if they did.'

He handed me a photo. It looked like it had been blown up from a holiday snap. She was squinting into the sun, grinning.

She had a wide attractive face, a large gap between her upper front teeth, lots of freckles and light brown hair with a kink in it which framed her face. She wore golden earrings and a necklace, a white blouse.

'Her hair's similar now?' I checked.

'Yes.'

'Dad?' Jacob put his head round the door.

'We're nearly done,' Mark said.

'Come in here, let's get you a drink,' I heard Trisha tell him.

'Are there any places Janet knows well, where she might go?'

'She's some family in Birmingham, but she doesn't like the place. Her dad's dead, her mother emigrated, they don't get on.'

'Holidays?'

He gave a harsh laugh. 'Fat chance! We used to go to Cornwall – camping. Not been anywhere the last couple of years. Bought this place just as prices were getting really silly. We could barely manage once I got the push.'

Gathering my papers together, I asked him if there was anything else. He hesitated, a barely perceptible pause. His lips moved then stilled. Then he said, 'No, nothing I can think of.' He didn't fool me. In that moment's hiatus he chose to conceal something from me.

There was one key difference in what I had learnt from Mark and what Trisha had told me about the missing woman. Trisha had been adamant that Janet was not seeing anyone but her husband thought she might be.

Once Jacob had re-joined his father in the living room I had chance to quiz Trisha about it again. She was washing pots at the kitchen sink.

'I'd know,' she said. 'She tells me everything. We confide in each other – always have.'

'How long have you known each other?'

'Fifteen years. If she was seeing anyone, met anyone, she'd have said.'

'Maybe she thought you'd disapprove?'

She gave a little laugh. Rinsed her hands and began to dry them. 'No. I was married before,' she volunteered by way of example, 'and so was Steve – we had an affair and I'd been playing around before that. If I hadn't been able to talk to Janet about it, I'd have gone mad. She's the same. Besides, when would she have had time for a lover? She worked full time, spent most night preparing lessons or filling in endless forms, she'd two kids and she did all the housework.' She lowered her voice even though we couldn't have been overheard. 'If Mark thinks Janet's having an affair, well, he's just clutching at straws. Trying to find an explanation. Any explanation. And he's wrong.'

She looked at me, head tilted to one side, her mouth pulled down in an expression of regret or sympathy. 'I wish he was right,' she added. 'Then it'd all make sense. But this,' she flapped the tea towel, 'this is bloody awful, I tell you.'

CHAPTER FOUR

Back at my office, I began sifting through the lists and notes and Janet's address book, to sort out who I would follow up. My time was Trisha Marlowe's money and I didn't think it prudent to retrace the steps that she and Mark had already taken. The people I wanted to talk to included Janet's dentist, her hairdresser, the yoga class she attended on Monday evenings and colleagues at the school where she'd been supply teaching.

Her address book was very old, dating back to her university days. Trisha was in there; her details crossed out and changed several times. Trisha Brackham who became Trisha Sheild and then Marlowe.

The exercise brought with it a sudden roll of déjà vu. I was thrown back years to the time of my father's death, when I'd sat in our hall with my mother, ringing round all their friends to break the news. It had been a curious task, painful but reassuring too, as my mother recounted anecdotes about people I barely knew or had never met. Conjuring up a picture of my father as a young man, a bachelor and then a young parent. 'Terry was in a band with your dad, a drummer. But he couldn't keep time when he'd had a few drinks so they were always trying to keep him away from the bar.' 'Leonie was his first girlfriend. She married a chef. They opened a place near Congleton. We had a holiday with them in Scotland. You'd have been about eighteen months. Toddling about.' And. 'Your dad loved William; they were more like brothers than cousins, up half the night swapping cricketing stories.'

I missed my dad, missed the fact that he'd never known Maddie. He'd have been a brilliant granddad. Ray's father was dead too, though his mother, Nana Tello, was very much alive and kicking. Stress the kicking. Thinking of Ray made my stomach reel. Fear or excitement? Different anyway from the heavy weight of tension in the preceding weeks. Last night's kiss had moved things on. I dragged my mind back to the task in hand and finalised my notes. Lunchtime.

When possible, I have lunch at home, it's one of the perks of being self-employed – though the downside is I have to make it myself. There was some hummus in the fridge and plenty of salad stuff. A warmed pitta bread and it was done. I took it outside to eat. The hole in the lawn looked awful, a scar on the landscape. The surrounding turf was still bruised and I had tracked mud all over the flagstones on the patio, too. The sooner the pit was lined and filled with water, the better.

While I ate, I watched the birds. There were magpies, with their black and white plumage, large, loud and flashy, crashing in and out of the trees and squawking at each other. We had sparrows too, blackbirds, a wren, a pair of robins and tits. Before I left, I measured the crater I'd dug, trying not to get too mucky in the process.

* * *

Longsight is one of the poorer neighbourhoods in Manchester. The low cost of housing there makes it popular with immigrant communities moving to work in the city: Irish, Eastern European, then Asian, West Indian, African. Cheek by jowl with Rusholme, where the thriving Indian restaurants are, Longsight is also home to some of the notorious drugs gangs and the site of several gang shootings. It's cycling distance from my home in Withington but I hoped to call at the garden centre as well if I got time and I couldn't carry what I wanted back on the bike.

Stockport Road was busy as I drove though the area. The Asian grocery stores with tables on the pavement and the bargain discount outlets were doing a roaring trade. If you wanted ten biros for a pound, a plastic mop and bucket or fresh coriander and dried fenugreek seeds it was the place to be. The parade of old buildings that housed the shops seemed to list to one side, with flaking paint, crumbling stonework and sagging roofs adding to the impression of decrepitude. A lot of the shops had slapped lurid colours and brash slogans over the frontages to create a cheerful impression – it worked if you didn't look too closely. The modern units further along looked even worse: cheap, offal-coloured brick and plastic-glass windows. Groups of people were out shopping: Asian women in shalwar kameez or saris, younger ones in Western dress, black families, clusters of white teenagers and elderly couples. And everywhere children and buggies.

Passing the library and the Pakistani Community Centre, I forked left. Here slum terraces had been replaced by slum semis. Soulless modern housing, built to tiny dimensions (though all the evidence showed each generation was larger than the last) with narrow windows that made me think of prisons and sieges.

I kept referring to my A–Z and found the street where Ramin was staying. His house was one of the newish ones and looked unoccupied. The windows were boarded up and a chain-link fence topped with coils of barbed wire surrounded it. The adjoining property made do with wooden paling, broken in places. I pushed open the gate in the chain link and knocked on the door. There was a spy hole and when I heard movement from inside, I wondered if Ramin was peering out to check it was me.

A child on a mountain bike paused at the edge of the road, looking my way. I glanced at him and he flicked a V-sign at me and then pumped his pedals and hurtled away.

There was the sound of bolts being drawn and Ramin let me in.

'Lot of security,' I said as I stepped into the tiny hall.

He gave a grin, a small shrug. 'I think the man before have...enemies. People still look for him.'

There were only two rooms downstairs, one at the front which Ramin told me was a bedroom and a kitchen-cum-living room at the back. Outside this, through sliding glass doors, was a patch of ground, not much bigger than a double bed. A broken rotary drying rack stood in the middle of it next to an upended child's sit and ride toy. Razor wire edged the fencing. I couldn't see any trees, just the silhouette of jagged metal thorns against the high, blue sky.

The room boasted a small television set balanced on a pine stool, a circular melamine table that had begun to bulge at the edges where damp must have got into the chipboard, four stacking polypropylene chairs, a foam sofa bed and a divan bed covered with ill-matched cushions. There was a Calor gas cooker on a short counter top besides a sink. And a fridge tucked underneath. A large poster of Manchester United adorned one wall. The room smelt of old cigarettes and cooking fat. Given the level of security, the windows probably wouldn't open.

'You a fan?' I nodded at the Reds poster.

'Yes,' a quick smile, 'but mostly I like to play. We have a team at the centre. Berfan is the top scorer. We could walk? I tell you about him.'

I agreed. A turn round the park beat sitting there, hands down.

It only took a few minutes to reach the small green space. We found a bench in the sunshine and sat. Ramin lit a cigarette, offered me one. I don't smoke. He sucked hard on his then blew the smoke out of his bottom lip so it drifted up his face like a veil. I told him that Berfan hadn't been admitted to any of the hospitals I'd rung. He took another pull on his cigarette.

'When did you last see Berfan?' I asked him.

'Sunday. The morning we play football, the afternoon I went to the centre Berfan said he's going to the house. When I got back he was gone.'

'Any ideas?'

'Sometimes there is work – at the big market or building. Cash. I ask the man who know about this but he says Berfan did not go there.'

'Anywhere else?'

'Trouble maybe? Or hiding?'

'He had his asylum application refused.'

'Yes, his appeal. No more chance.' He dragged hard on the cigarette. 'He can't go back,' he said simply. 'I can't go back.'

'You've been refused too?'

'Not yet.' His tone told me what he expected.

Rachel had told me that many of the people she was campaigning for never had the chance to argue their case, that decisions were still being made without the authorities being fully appraised of the facts behind someone's flight here.

'If they deport you?'

'They won't.' He leant forward bracing his elbows on his knees. 'I will go to London, Birmingham.'

'But your brother – if he's hiding and I try to find him, that's the last thing he's going to want.'

'I know this. I do not bring him trouble but maybe he already has problem with the police.'

'I can certainly check to see if he's in custody.'

I frowned. I was about to ask him why his brother might have been picked up and detained when he explained.

'Berfan is small,' he levelled his hand by his own jaw, 'brave. But he never run away. He fights back. Sometimes it is better not to be so brave.'

Brave or belligerent? Did Berfan go round picking fights? Stirring things up? Asylum seekers, like any other group of people, would include a small proportion of criminals, thieves, rapists, people prone to violence. Was Berfan one of them?

Ramin tapped the filter end of his cigarette with his thumb and continued: 'When they take us, in Iran, they hurt us. Berfan he never say what they want to know.'

I sat still, my mind grappling with the circumstances he described. A world glimpsed in documentaries and news reports but way beyond my own experience.

'What did they want?'

'Names, confessions, lies.'

He stood up abruptly and walked a few paces away. I stayed where I was, watching the traffic pass beyond the railings and a toddler crowing with delight at a stranger's dog. The dog, unnerved by such boundless affection, hid behind its owner prompting the child to run after it.

Ramin looked ashen when he came back to the bench.

'Shall we head back?' I said.

He tried to smile but his eyes were soft with pain.

There were three men in the room at the house when we returned. The television was on, an afternoon chat show with atrocious reception. Half the picture was awash with a red hue. Ramin spoke to the men, telling them what I was doing there, I assume.

'How many of you live here?' I asked him.

'Officially?' He grinned.

I smiled back.

'We keep warm,' he said ironically.

'I need a good description of Berfan,' I told him, 'and his details.'

He gave me his full name, Berfan Yalik and his date of birth. I asked him for the photo.

He said something to one of the other men who went out and returned with a Polaroid. Three men and a football.

'Here.' Ramin pointed to the central figure. I could see the family likeness, a strong nose, pointed jaw line, Berfan was slighter and shorter than Ramin. The other man, the one who'd brought the picture and completed the trio in the snapshot, towered over them both.

'How tall is Berfan?'

'I am one eighty,' Ramin said and looked to his friends. 'Berfan?' He moved his hand up and down his own face.

'One seventy,' one said.

'What was he wearing?'

'Jeans, a Manchester United shirt – an old grey one. Jacket. Trainers.'

'Glasses?' I pointed to my eyes.

He shook his head. One of the others said something quickly and they all laughed.

'They say I am the one who wants glasses,' Ramin translated. 'I miss penalty on Sunday.'

'Jewellery?'

'Gold chain,' he traced a line around his neck, 'not real.'

'Anything else? Tattoos, marks?'

His face sank. 'Yes.' He glanced down at the table, pressing his fist against it. 'Many. His legs, his feet, his belly,' he brought his hands to gesture the length of his body. 'All over. Cuts, burns. Many, many marks.'

CHAPTER FIVE

The basement room that I lease from the family who occupy the rest of the building is only a couple of minutes from my home. With one phone call to central switchboard at the police headquarters, I established that Berfan wasn't being held in custody at a police station and hadn't been remanded on bail.

Hopefully, Ramin would be relieved. His little brother hadn't ended up fighting, standing his ground perhaps and getting arrested or beaten for his pains. The way Ramin described Berfan's injuries haunted me. Had Ramin himself been tortured like that? Wasn't that experience reason enough to grant asylum? I had told Ramin that I'd get back to him the next day – sooner if I had news. He had my number in case he heard from Berfan.

At half past two, I switched on my answerphone, locked up and set out for the garden centre. Timing it just right, I brought back a sheet of pond liner and went on from there to school. Tom came out before Maddie. He'd inherited Ray's wavy, black hair and Mediterranean complexion. He was as skinny as a stick.

'Jacket,' I reminded him and he turned on one heel and ran

back in. 'And your kit!' I called after him.

He emerged later carrying both. Maddie found us and we wove our way through the playground, steering round a small red-faced child, prone and in the throes of a stupendous tantrum and past a family with baby triplets in a state-of-the-art buggy.

'Did you get Cheerios?' Tom looked up at me.

'I've not been shopping today. I didn't get any yesterday.'

His shoulders slumped. 'Did Dad go?'

'I don't think so.'

'You only want them because of the spaceships,' Maddie put in.

'And they taste nice,' Tom said.

'Well, we'll put them on the list for next time.'

We lingered by the municipal flowerbed near the bus stop while they each had a turn at running all the way round the low brick wall. Tom moved more quickly than Maddie. He'd always been the more physically able child; she the more careful. The flowerbed was planted up each season with a different design. This time they'd used marigolds, busy lizzies and various thyme varieties to create a picture of a boat.

When we got home, I gave the kids a snack of milk and toast and tried to persuade them to play out. The weather was fine but they preferred the telly.

Ray was working late; he did four days a week for an advertising company, a fairly recent move. His package includes extra holidays, unpaid, so he can look after Tom. When he works overtime, I do extra childcare. By the same token, if my work suddenly gets frantic I ask him to do more of the school runs or we pay a babysitter to pick them up. We always have to negotiate it which is a good position to be in – no one's taken for granted.

I emptied the dishwasher, then swept and mopped the kitchen floor, displacing Digger in the process. He slunk out into the hall.

Making tea, I listened to the radio. The situation in Iraq still dominated the headlines. Along with millions of others, I'd opposed the war – and lost. Now that the country continued to be torn apart and terrorism escalated elsewhere there was no sense of vindication just sadness and anger. I flipped stations until I heard a snatch of music that appealed, some Blur from the Britpop days.

At nine o' clock, I was settling down to a couple of pints with my friend Diane in our regular pub.

'You're looking better.' Diane knew me well and had helped support me through a tough time after a particularly devastating case. She was right. I was much better. The flashbacks had stopped. I was sleeping well. But perhaps my demeanour lay with the new development. Thinking of Ray I felt my face alter with embarrassment.

'What?' She didn't miss a trick.

'Nothing,' I began but could see that she wasn't going to wear it. 'It's ridiculous.'

'What?! Don't go all coy on me. You've met someone?'

'No.' That would have been so much easier. 'It's… erm…well, a while back, Ray, there was a moment,' speaking quickly in my rush to explain, 'I don't know what else to call it, a moment – this sudden attraction...' My face blazed. 'I don't know why, I was really upset, he...'

'Ray?' Diane's eyes were huge with consternation, her mouth curved in astonishment.

I ran my hands through my hair. 'Nothing happened, hardly anything happened.'

'When? Why didn't you tell me?' She drew herself up. Diane is what they call statuesque and she thrust everything my way.

'I was going to. It was when work was crazy and, I don't know, we got interrupted, and then...well, it was just a blip.'

'A blip,' she said incredulously.

'A delusion.'

'And?'

I hesitated.

'You've slept with him. You've been to bed with him.'

'No!' I scowled. There was a faint 'not yet' echoing somewhere in my head.

'Blimey, Sal.' She regarded me. 'And that's it – a moment?'

'And last night we kissed,' I said quickly.

'Kissed?' Contemptuously.

'Snogged, then. God, I hate that word.'

'You and Ray.' She shook her head.

'Me too,' I echoed her disbelief.

'Well, who started it?' she demanded.

'I don't know. It's just so odd. We've been living in that place together nearly six years – it feels like I'm falling for my cousin or something.'

'Are you?'

'What?'

'Falling for him?'

I sighed and took a long drink. 'It felt good,' I finally spoke, 'physically.'

She raised her eyebrows, her eyes gleamed.

'But the rest: he's moody, he's got a moustache...'

'Buy him a razor,' she said.

I burst out laughing. 'It's not that, it's – there's so much riding on it. The house, the kids...' That worried me more than anything, the prospect of breaking up our 'family'.

'But that's always been a possibility,' she pointed out. 'When he was seeing Laura you thought they might move out.' She stopped, looked sharply at me. 'Is this why he finished with her?'

I nodded, feeling guilty,

'So, he's serious?'

'I don't know what to do, Diane. I don't know if we're suited in that way. Whether I could love him, properly.'

'What are your options?'

'Stop it now. Sit him down and tell him I'm not interested. And he might walk out, anyway, then.'

'Or?'

'Go with the flow.'

After a minute, she spoke again. 'Take him to bed. It's not like you're marrying the guy. People do that, you know, sleep together then end up agreeing to remain friends.'

'How? Who?' I demanded. How come other people could keep things so simple. Crikey, all we'd done is share one kiss and already I was caught in a web of emotional uncertainties.

'Lots of people. And it might be the real thing.'

The real thing? 'Didn't think we believed in *the real thing*.'

'When it suits.' She grinned. She gave a little laugh and drained her glass. 'You and Ray,' she repeated, shaking her head.

'Same again?'

While the bartender pulled our pints, I studied the banknotes from around the world pinned up behind the bar in between the Irish knick-knacks and Greek plates. The landlord was from Athens, his wife from Dublin. Every so often, they talked about moving to one or the other. I hoped they'd never get round to it. They maintained a typical old-fashioned English pub, warm and inviting. A snug for sitting and talking, a taproom with games in dominated by men but not exclusively so. Excellent beer, no gimmicks. Music was only played if someone fed the jukebox and the volume was kept at a reasonable level so you could still hold a conversation. There was no telly.

Sitting back down next to Diane, I rummaged in my bag, putting the change away. 'What about you, then? What's new?'

'Nothing good.' The unusual flat tone in her voice made me turn towards her. She had a peculiar look on her face. 'I went to the hospital today, got my results. It's cancer.' Her mouth wobbled. 'I've got breast cancer. They've caught it early, they say, I've a good chance.' She took a breath. 'So,' she went on briskly, 'no need to get the ham out, yet.'

'Oh, Diane.' I put my arm round her and hugged her close, squashing my own shock and panic. And I listened as she told me all about it.

CHAPTER SIX

My dreams were filled with anxiety: water was flooding through the house, sweeping everything before it, the roof crumbling, terror ripping through me as I remembered I'd left a corpse in the cellar and they'd find me out. Then I was on stage. I was in a costume, I was supposed to be singing. Nobody had warned me I had to sing. I didn't know the words. And I was late to fetch the children from school. I woke with a lurch. The images still fresh. It didn't take an analyst to work out what had triggered them.

Before work, I cycled down to Didsbury, where there are more fancy shops than in Withington, and wandered up the main street looking for something for Diane. There were some beautiful earrings that would suit her, glass coloured like amber, held in a silver spiral. I'd a brief image of her balding from chemo, wearing flamboyant scarves. She'd need some nice earrings. I chided myself for being melodramatic. Diane didn't know yet exactly what treatment she would get or how it would affect her. She was going back to the hospital the following week and I'd go with her. Choosing a card, I walked back and stopped off at the Cheese Hamlet. Made up a mini-hamper of delicacies for her: olives, cheeses, coffee, biscuits, she loved her food. I got them to vacuum pack anything leaky then I took it all to the Post Office, packed it in a carton and posted it.

Trying to find a trail for Janet Florin was my mission for the day. Over the phone, I spoke to her dentist and optician. Neither had seen her recently. I didn't have a phone number for the yoga class she attended but I knew the venue – it was where I went to my self-defence classes. The yoga group met on a Monday so I'd wait and call in then.

It's a cliché that hairdressers are awash with gossip but it's one that holds some truth. Janet got her hair cut at a salon in Chorlton, a cosmopolitan area just south of where they lived. Her stylist, though a little unsure, agreed to see me before her eleven o' clock appointment.

The place was nicely done out, beech skirting boards and furnishings, dusky rose walls with well-designed track lighting, large mirrors, each set at an angle so clients could concentrate on their own reflection and not everyone else's. Allie was a pert, blonde woman with tiny, rectangular glasses and a large, swollen belly; heavily pregnant. There was another hairdresser shampooing a customer when I arrived, and Allie took me through to the staffroom at the back. Accepting her offer of a cup of tea, I chatted to her about the pregnancy while she fixed our drinks (it was her first, she was six months along, knackered and she'd found her first varicose vein – a hazard of the profession anyway).

'I checked the book,' she said, 'and it was the Saturday before last Janet was in.' A few days before she went missing.

'How was she?' I asked.

'Fine. When you said that she'd walked out, well, I was surprised.'

'There may have been another man.'

She screwed up her mouth. 'Not that I ever heard of.'

'Did she talk about her marriage?'

'A bit. I know her husband had lost his job, he'd been stressed with all that, you know. She thought they might have to sell up and move.'

'Did she seem worried?' Perhaps the pressure of money worries had come to dominate Janet's thoughts and had precipitated her leaving the family.

Allie thought for a moment. 'The opposite really, quite upbeat, more bubbly than she had been.' She stopped. 'She left the kids?'

I nodded. She made an expression of dismay. 'That's not on,' she said. Then she looked puzzled. 'She talked about them all the time.'

'What did she say at that last appointment – can you remember?'

She pulled a face. 'Erm…the little boy had a birthday party he was going to – fancy dress…and work, she was finishing at this school – she said it had been a nightmare, kids off the wall.'

'Perhaps that was why she was happier?'

'Could be.' She rubbed her hand on her stomach then stopped and patted at it subconsciously. 'When I think about it now…' She grinned and broke off. 'No, it sounds daft.'

'No, go on, please.' I'm a firm believer in hunches and intuition; so much of what we 'know' is unspoken, gleaned rather than stated, working at a deeper level of communication.

'Well, now you've told me she's gone off, it makes me think she was planning it. She was excited more than happy.' She frowned. 'And she didn't make her next appointment. We usually put it in each time, six weeks ahead, always have. Saturdays are busy so it makes sense with her teaching to make sure I can fit her in. Anyway, she said something about not knowing where she'd be working next and she'd leave it and ring me. But that doesn't make sense. She'd still need a Saturday unless she stopped teaching altogether. And with her husband's situation, that'd be a bit daft.'

I saw exactly what she was getting at. Janet was a supply teacher; wherever she worked she would still be off at the weekends. Breaking the routine of her hair appointments was the biggest indication I had so far that there might have been some foresight to Janet's disappearance. If she had been seeing someone (big if) then they could have been planning to elope. But why such secrecy? Because the only way she could deal with leaving her children was to completely sever all ties? Because she felt that was fairer to them than the pain of knowing where she was and that she had chosen to abandon them? *She'd never leave them*, Trisha had said. But women do. We find it shocking, the severing of the bond between mother and child, a reversal of all the myths about motherhood. But some mothers leave.

Force of habit made me think of other explanations for the nuggets of information I'd garnered. Janet's mood could still be linked to escape from the job she loathed. The delicious prospect of waking in the morning without that coil of dread in her belly. Or perhaps she'd started taking vitamins, or practised her yoga more and was feeling chirpier as a result.

And the hair appointment? Money was still an issue for the Florins, even more so with Janet having a break from her supply teaching. Perhaps she needed to economise, let her hair grow and save the £25 a time.

If Janet had been planning to leave Mark, she hadn't spoken about it to anyone close. Might she have told a colleague at work? Telling a relative stranger reduces the risk of word getting back to her husband. She hadn't taken anything with her though, just her handbag and the clothes she stood up in. Although Mark couldn't be sure what those were.

I thanked Allie for her time and wished her luck with the baby. Driving back along Mauldeth Road West, I got stuck at roadworks; temporary traffic lights forced us to queue. The car ahead of me tried to race through on red and met an oncoming taxi. There was a savage squeal of brakes but they didn't actually crash. For a moment, it looked like there would be a brawl, with the taxi driver gesticulating, winding his window down and shouting and the other bloke cursing and jabbing his finger at him. But once the barking was done, the taxi swung round the other car and drove on.

It was another fine day, the central reservation was thick with dandelions and daisies, the trees along the edge of the playing field were lush and leafy, spilling shade across the road. An elderly woman, her back bent over, a Zimmer frame in her hands, made her way, bit by bit along the pavement. I wondered where she was going and whether she was relishing the summer day as I was. Was this a daily journey she was making or something out of the ordinary? A chance to take the air and smell the flowers or a tedious chore?

The traffic lights changed and I moved forward towards the junction where another huge apartment block was being thrown up. *BUY NOW!* screamed the hoardings. *Luxury Apartments, only a few remaining.* They are always luxury apartments, aren't they? Never standard or basic or no-frills. Doesn't matter how small they are – and some of them give new meaning to the word petite – or what quality the fittings, they are all branded luxury.

One other thing struck me about Janet's reported mood. In general, people who leave home tend to do so from a position of unhappiness, despair, a sense of isolation. They are low and the only solution they can see is to flee. The picture of Janet as excited and bubbly, suggested she might have been going to something rather than just running away from something. What or who or where? And why hadn't she taken any luggage?

My mobile rang a couple of minutes later and I pulled over to take the call. I have a hands-free set but I don't often use it. My concentration is better if I'm not clocking all the other traffic and looking out for the dodgy drivers.

'Have you heard anything?' asked Bob Swithinbank.

I smiled at the urgency in his voice. 'She'll only just have got the letter.'

He sighed. 'Yeah.'

The adoption enquiries I do are among the most rewarding but also the most sensitive of my cases. Sandra Patefield, Bob's birth mother, may well have not told anyone that she had given a baby boy up for adoption. We didn't know anything about her life, whether she was married or had other children.

'You know it's important that we don't rush things,' I

reminded him. 'We're more likely to have a positive outcome if we take it at a pace everyone is easy with.'

'What if she's away? Or if she's moved?'

'Let's give it a few days, then I'll think about a follow-up.'

'You could ring her, see if she got the letter?'

'They're not listed, could be ex-directory.'

'Oh, no,' he groaned.

'I know it's hard to wait but it's been thirty years, Bob, another few weeks, maybe a couple of months, they're not going to make much difference. If I hear anything at all, I'll let you know straightaway.'

'OK,' he said resignedly.

How's the tour?'

'Wild! Barriers all over the place. Sometimes I don't know if we're doing a rock concert or a political rally.'

I laughed. A couple of years previously, Crashbucket had released an anti-war song called 'Threats and Promises', a melodic rock-anthem, all thrashing beat and Bob's gravelly vocals mixing with soaring vocal harmonies from the backing singers. With lyrics like: *Bush bagged Baghdad, ran 'em ragged, ran 'em sad, bombed the good and the bad. Blood and oil, oil and blood. This ain't freedom, this ain't peace. Just war. Not a just war. Just a Bush war.* It wasn't subtle but it had sold like wildfire and they couldn't perform anywhere without playing it – and attracting anti-war demonstrators.

Reassuring him that I'd let him know the minute I heard so much as a whisper from Sandra, I wished him well for the rest of the tour.

Fixing lunch at home, I found myself musing on babies. There was Allie, the hairdresser, expecting a baby who would surely change her life for ever. Then Bob, no baby now, but when Sandra Patefield read that letter it would catapult her back thirty years to the time when she had relinquished her baby. And Janet Florin's babies, now five and eight. I could understand her leaving Mark, to be honest, I found it hard to work out what she had seen in him, but the kids – how tough that must be.

CHAPTER SEVEN

Arriving at Ramin's house, I was struck again by the savage security; a sad little fortress. What had the previous occupant been? A drug-dealer, a debt-collector? Ramin let me in. I told him that Berfan hadn't been arrested, at least not in or around Manchester.

He nodded. 'Someone saw him,' he said. 'This morning they tell me at the centre: someone saw him on Monday. There's a place you go for work, hard work.'

'Casual work?' I'd seen images on the television: gangs packed into vans for a day, picking crops or shifting rubble.

'Yes.'

'Can I talk to this person?'

'Yes.' He slipped his jacket on.

In the car, he patted the dashboard. 'Nice. What engine?'

'Don't know,' I said. '1200? 1300?' I'd never cared much for cars, no interest in them. However, I'd had to learn a bit for my job, enough to be able to recognise make and model when I was tracing or trailing people. Knowing they 'drove a blue car with a sloping back' wouldn't swing it in the world of surveillance so I swotted up – but knowing engine size was a step too far.

'I fix cars,' Ramin said, 'at home.'

'You're a mechanic?'

He nodded. 'I have garage.'

He seemed so young to have his own business. 'What about Berfan?'

'Berfan was training for engineer – at university.'

In the pause that followed, I wondered whether to ask any more questions. Was it something Ramin wanted to talk about or something best dealt with by forgetting?

'Here.' He pointed left showing me where to turn.

We drew up outside a large detached Victorian house. A fading mural decorated the wall that ran along the front garden. The gateposts each boasted a lion though one had lost its head. There was a plethora of signboards in the garden, advertising the different organisations that had a base on the premises.

Ramin took me up to a door at the side where he pressed an intercom. He gave his name and we were buzzed in.

The Welcome Centre had a suite of rooms on the ground floor. We went through one, cluttered with tables and chairs and busy with people (all men) playing chess or cards or reading and talking. Going by appearances, most of them were Middle Eastern, with colouring similar to Ramin's. The snatches of language I heard sounded like his, too.

Ramin spoke briefly to one of the men and gestured to me that we all needed to go to another room. Here there were three women, two of them holding babies. The women wore headscarves and long loose robes. A toddler was sitting close to the small television set, reaching out and pointing to things on the screen.

There was a kitchen area in one corner where a bird-like

woman with grey hair and scrawny arms was serving toasted sandwiches and hot drinks to a couple of young men and talking to them in a strong Mancunian accent.

Ramin led us to three low armchairs grouped round a coffee table. He spoke to the man in English, then introduced me. The man had dull, very dark skin, slate grey hair, his teeth were broken and yellowed. He nodded politely.

'Yes,' he said to me, 'Berfan was at the pick-up in the line.'

I looked at Ramin for explanation.

'If you want to work you stand in line. They see – how strong, how big.'

'Did you talk to him?' I asked the other man.

'Just hello. Then he's fighting.'

'Who with?'

'One of the other boys. I think Berfan was pushing for a good place, someone pushed back. He was shouting. People put him out of the way.'

'Was he hurt?'

The man shrugged. 'A little only.'

I'd noticed one of the mothers was intent on our conversation. She came over to us, bobbed her head in greeting and spoke quickly to Ramin. I heard the name Berfan.

'She says she saw him also. On Tuesday.' Ramin said.

The woman spoke some more. Ramin translated. 'Tuesday afternoon, he was in town near the fountains in the gardens. She says he looked...sad.' Ramin put his hands to his head. 'Like this. And he was there again on Wednesday.'

Two days ago.

What she said next made him flush lightly, brought a spark of irritation into his eyes.

'He was begging,' Ramin told me. 'The police move him away.'

The older man made a tutting sound though I don't know whether his disapproval was for Berfan or the police. The woman inclined her head and returned to her seat.

'Can you tell us anything else about the fight?' I asked the man. 'Do you know the other boy?'

'No. It was all over very quickly and Berfan left.'

A simple scrap, soon forgotten or had Berfan made an enemy that day? Someone who would bide his time and then get his own back. Had he caught up with Berfan since? Berfan would be unlikely to report any attack – with his asylum application rejected and considering whether to evade deportation, he'd not want the police asking too many questions.

As we left the centre, Ramin tried to make sense of Berfan's behaviour. 'Wednesday – she saw him Wednesday. Where is he sleeping? Why is he not at the house?'

'We should go there, into town,' I said, 'see if he's there again – if people have seen him.'

'Now?'

'Yes.'

It's only ten minutes from Longsight into town – and another ten finding parking. In the end, I shelled out for an NCP space instead of driving round any longer hoping for a meter.

The city centre is in constant redevelopment. The IRA bombing in 1996 had rewritten the scale and scope of building work and the Commonwealth Games added to it. And it kept on rolling. You can't cast an eye at the Manchester skyline anymore without spotting a flock of

cranes, can't walk quarter of a mile without passing wooden
hoardings shielding the latest crater from view. The newest
big project was the Beetham Tower, a 47-storey skyscraper
on Deansgate, way higher than anything else and visible from
miles away.

We walked up to Piccadilly Gardens which has had its
makeover. The old formal flowerbed and benches had been
replaced by an innovative grid of fountains, which bubbled up
and down randomly among stepping stones set in the floor. A
child magnet. And enjoyed by those who'd had a skinful, on
occasions. There was green space with trees. One end of the
square had been flogged off, the public space now encroached
upon by a private development: a four-storey brick building
that obscured the ornate Victoriana of the hotel behind which
had matched the grandeur of the row of old buildings along
Piccadilly itself.

'They are making something here?' Ramin gestured to the
curving concrete wall that the council had erected along one
edge of the area.

I laughed. 'I think that's it. Horrible, isn't it?' When it
had first gone up, I'd imagined they would decorate it with
mosaics perhaps. Or grow climbing plants? Or commission
bas-relief to reflect the lively, sometimes bloody history of
the place. They'd done nothing. The wall remained a paean
to concrete. Its only redeeming feature was the fact it
curved. The grey, slab-like aspect of it reminded me of a
thousand housing estates, of high rises, and bleak
municipal addresses, of car parks and subways stinking of
urine.

As we rounded the end of it, there was a man scrubbing off

graffiti. The message was still legible: KEEP ENGLAND
WHITE. I saw Ramin glance at it, and his mouth tighten a
little in response.

I had Berfan's photo and we asked some of the people
dotted around if they'd seen him.

A paper seller remembered him being moved on by the police.
'Gives the place a bad name, begging. They're coming down
hard on it these days.'

'When was this?'

'Yesterday, I saw him. Thursday.'

Ramin looked at me; hope brightened his expression, made
him appear even younger.

'What happened?'

'He was messing about, like. Getting down on his knees,
being awkward. It's not right though, is it? Begging in this day
and age.' He grimaced with disapproval. Nipped the end of
his cigarette and tucked away what was left. 'They gave him
the old soft-shoe shuffle. Sent him packing.'

No one else we approached could tell us anything. 'We
know he's not being held by the police,' I reminded Berfan.
'The best thing would be to talk to the ones that moved him
on yesterday; they might be able to help.'

Ramin swallowed and thrust his hands deeper into his
jacket. He was nervous, I assumed, and didn't relish an
encounter with the police. Perhaps his dealings with them here
had been tricky or perhaps the prospect brought back
memories of the police back home who had been party to his
imprisonment and bad treatment.

'There'll be regular patrols in town,' I told him. 'Leave it to
me, I'll see who I can find – we can meet back here in half an

hour.' I found a fiver in my bag and handed it to him. 'You could get a coffee.'

He shook his head. I thought he was refusing the money.

'I can put it on expenses,' I told him.

'It is all right,' he said. 'I will come with you.'

We found a pair of officers near the Metro Link platform at the top of Market Street. Once they'd heard me out, they used their two-way radio to track down the officers who had actually dealt with Berfan.

We waited. The pedestrianised area was thronged with people. At intervals stood individuals clutching clipboards and wearing matching jackets. They were accosting passers-by. 'Accident, love? Any falls, any accidents, mate?' Trying to drum up takers for compensation claims. They had scant success. It looked like a soulless job and the man closest to me had a pinched look and wore run-down trainers and trousers a little too short. Did they get commission? Did they get the minimum wage?

After a few minutes, a female officer arrived, Constable Naylor.

'He was contravening the bye-laws,' she said. She couldn't have been more than twenty with a soft, slack look as though she was only part-baked. 'He mucked about a bit when we told him to move on.'

'Where did he go?'

'We escorted him to Dale Street – away from the shoppers. Told him not to show his face for a while. He'd been told once already.'

I glanced at Ramin. His face darkened, I couldn't tell whether it was anger or embarrassment.

'You've not seen him today?'

She shook her head.

That was where the trail dried up.

'We're a bit closer,' I told Ramin after she'd gone. 'I'm afraid I need to get back now but it might be worth walking round town, see if he's hanging around. You could try near the Town Hall, St Ann's Square, Exchange Square – anywhere that's busy. He might be sleeping rough or got a place in the Men's Hostel.'

Ramin jerked his head in frustration. 'Why?' he demanded. He didn't expect an answer. He made a gesture towards himself, then away, then back to himself. The message was clear: they'd been together, two brothers. Now Berfan had abandoned him.

'You're close?' I gave him the chance to talk about it.

'Some time,' he replied quietly. There was regret in his tone and the choice of words seemed odd. Did he mean they used to be close but weren't any longer? Or that their closeness fluctuated?

'Have you argued? Has there been bad feeling between you and Berfan? And now he's gone?' Was a row between the brothers part of the background to all this?

His gaze turned cold. 'No.'

An awkward pause followed. He looked away across the parade of people streaming by, to the shop windows on the other side of the street.

'OK then,' I said briskly, 'are you all right for getting back?'

'It's not far.'

'If you want the bus fare—'

'No. Thank you.'

Polite enough but I could tell I'd upset him. There wasn't anything I could do about it – especially as I wasn't sure exactly what my mistake had been.

After arranging to review the situation after the weekend, I said my goodbyes and left. In spite of the tension between us, I was feeling quite chirpy. We'd established that Berfan was alive and well and still in Manchester. Pretty good going for a couple of hours' work.

CHAPTER EIGHT

Tom and Ray were away for the weekend, a long-planned trip to the Lake District to visit an old friend of Ray's who lived up there.

Over the weekend, I made good progress on the pond. First thing Saturday, I started lining the hole with a layer of sand and then some old carpet.

'Is that to keep it warm?' Maddie asked.

'No, it's to stop any stones poking through the liner.'

'Can we have a fountain?'

'I haven't got a pump. We'd have to buy a pump and then plug it in so we'd need a channel from here to the house. It's a bit complicated. It'll be nice just still, like a little lake.'

She screwed up her face. 'A fountain would be better.'

'Ah, well,' I sat back on my heels. 'The thing is, a fountain makes that splashing noise, makes you want to wee all the time.'

She giggled then pretended to be affronted. At seven years old going on eight, she had to contend with an endless barrage of scatological remarks from the boys in her class at school. Like countless generations before them, they thought there was nothing more hilarious than references to body parts and toilet functions. Tom, a year younger, could be reduced to insensible giggling by the mention of the word bum alone.

Maddie helped me pull the liner over the hole and manoeuvre it until the largest overlap was beside the deepest section. The hole I'd dug was shallow at one end to help the local wildlife get in and out. The last thing I wanted to do was be responsible for drowned hedgehogs or shrews. Were there still shrews in the city? Rats yes. Squirrels yes, frogs and hedgehogs OK – but shrews?

I pushed the liner in and then turned the hose on to begin filling it. With the weight of the water, it stretched to fit the shape I'd excavated.

In one corner of the garden there had been a low stone wall – only a foot or so high – which must have been a raised bed. I'd dismantled it three or four years before when we were creating a level play area for the kids. The large flat-topped stones had been worth keeping. I'd stored them behind the shed and they were perfect for edging the pond and holding the liner in place. Using the wheelbarrow, I moved them across the garden four or five at a time. Then I spent ages trying them in various positions so that they fitted snugly together and the variations in height between the slabs didn't look too obvious. Even though it was a warm day, my fingers were soon numb and red with cold.

After lunch, Maddie stayed inside. I finished trimming the liner and then began dumping earth and some smaller stones in the pond to provide a seabed. It looked like a muddy soup, barren and raw. But in my imagination, creeping thyme filled the cracks between the stones, delicate reeds and rushes fringed the water and a 'beach' of pebbles gave the froglets somewhere to bask. With a dragonfly hovering above the clear azure water, my fantasy was complete.

I could barely walk by the time I'd finished. My back had seized up and my forearms ached, my legs were wobbly. A hot soak was the answer. This was accompanied by a soundtrack from Maddie who perched outside the bathroom door (a new prudish phase) and regaled me with choice pickings from her joke book.

Diane came round for a meal on Saturday evening. We tucked into Mediterranean roast vegetables, couscous and chickpea salad. Maddie ate four chickpeas, a few spoons of couscous and got herself ready for bed. Diane and I chatted but we didn't talk about her cancer. She had brought a video round. 'Not *Love Story*,' she joshed me. 'Male mid-life crises and wine drinking.' It was *Sideways*. 'You could pick up some tips for Ray.'

'You think that's what it is – his mid-life crisis?'

She shrugged. 'I haven't a clue.'

It should have been like any other night when we'd stayed in and shared a few glasses of wine, easy in each other's company. But it wasn't. Lingering beneath it was anxiety writ large. It seemed to me like we were both trying to be as normal, as ordinary, as possible, while we still could. Because there was a bloody great unknown looming.

Ray and Tom arrived home late on Sunday afternoon. I heard the car and felt my pulse swoop. Tom and Digger came bounding in and Maddie dragged Tom out to see the pond. Ray appeared, his arms full of sleeping bags and pillows. His hair was tousled and his skin darker from being outdoors. He smiled, nothing guarded about it, his eyes were bright, his teeth gleaming.

'Hello,' I said.

'Thought we'd eat out,' he said, 'treat the kids.'

I hesitated, surprised at the suggestion, it wasn't something we did very often. 'Sure, yes.'

He looked at me a while longer, warmth in his eyes until I looked away. And found myself smiling. He dipped his head and left carrying the stuff.

Just sleep with him, Diane had said. But since when had Diane been wise counsel? Although we were very close friends, she'd been in some messy relationships, which I'd been keen to see her end, but she had still gone back for more. And she'd been hurt. So in affairs of the heart she wasn't exactly my role model.

The four of us walked down to a place in Withington that did tapas and simple meals. All the time, I was conscious of Ray's proximity, physically hypersensitive. I tried not to brush against him in case he took it as an invitation. Neurotic, I thought to myself, this is making me neurotic.

Once we were seated and had given our orders for pizza and mixed tapas, I distracted myself talking to the kids.

'Did you have a good time, Tom?'

He nodded. 'We went on a boat and we had sausages for breakfast and Digger ate a frog.'

'Ewww!' Maddie protested.

'A big one and its leg was hanging out.'

'Enough,' Ray said.

'I hope he won't eat our frogs,' I said

'Have we got frogs?'

'We will have. Once they find that pond.'

As we chattered, my thoughts turned to Janet Florin and her two children. Was she missing them? And what about them? The little girl probably just felt a horrible loneliness because Mummy had gone away. But Jacob was old enough to try to find explanations, justifications. Perhaps to blame himself like so many children do when things go wrong for their parents.

Walking home, with the kids running ahead, I told Ray about Diane. 'They've caught it early,' I explained. 'There's a good chance of successful treatment.'

'Chemo?'

'I don't know. I'm not sure what order it all happens in. I'm going in to the hospital with her this week, they'll tell her then.'

He exhaled and shook his head at the news. Then his mobile went off.

'My mother,' he grimaced as he checked the display. 'Mama?'

The conversation was pretty one sided, with Ray nodding and attempting to say something now and again but that was par for the course with Nana Tello.

'Mama, it won't be a mouse. Try turning it off and on... OK, OK, I'll come round in a bit. Bye.' He turned to me. 'Her television's squeaking, she thinks there's a mouse inside.'

'Go now,' I suggested. 'I'll bath them.'

''Kay.'

He was ages. I began to be impatient, then worried. I considered ringing but that felt intrusive. At last, I heard Digger scrabble to his feet in the kitchen and trot to the door.

Our early warning system. I set my book aside and shuffled into a more comfortable position. But Ray didn't come in to see me, he whistled for Digger and took him out for a walk.

Sick at myself for mooning around like a besotted fifteen-year-old, I tried to figure out what I wanted. Was I ready to sleep with him – handle all the complications that would bring? Could it be worse than this state of suspense?

I cleared up the kitchen and turned things off in the lounge. I was heading upstairs when Ray got back.

'Find any mice?'

He grinned, hung up his jacket. 'The squeaking was the smoke alarm. Mind you, her telly is on the way out – and she'd got half a dozen plugs running off one socket.' He yawned, rubbed at the stubble on his chin.

There was a brief pause. If he touches me, I thought, if he makes a move, reaches out and touches me, I'll do it.

'G'night,' he said.

'Night.' The disappointment I felt told me everything I needed to know.

CHAPTER NINE

The school where Janet Florin had been working as a supply teacher was in a disadvantaged area of Stockport. The entrance hall was welcoming enough, with wildlife displays and lots of poems and drawings about ladybirds and dragonflies and one of those posters that extols the virtues of showing love and praise to children.

I hadn't made an appointment to see the staff. Experience had taught me that it's almost as hard to book to see a teacher as it is to see a doctor. I didn't want to wait days for a convenient slot. Five minutes impromptu chat at break time would be just as good.

The secretary didn't like it much but I carried on being persistent yet pleasant. What tipped it was the arrival of a harassed parent and a very distraught child. The boy was trying to prise himself away from her grasp and swearing loudly. The secretary hustled me to the staffroom to wait for break. I sat on one of the low easy chairs that edged the room. The centre of the space was filled with coffee tables pushed together. Strewn across the middle of these was a selection of books, toys and gadgets which the staff could buy at discount prices. The walls were awash with union and PTA notices and a whiteboard held notes about playground duty and after-school activities: *Fun Spanish starts next week, Samba Band every Mon, Wed till half term, Gill has the trip money for Air Raid Shelters.*

From where I sat, I could hear a teacher berating her class. The volume and venom of her delivery made my stomach shrink. I knew she was probably struggling with too many children and not enough support. It is hard to maintain discipline in such a situation without raising your voice but even so, it called up in me familiar feelings from my own childhood: the sick panic of being pinioned by that random rage. Maddie had a shouter one term at school, a supply teacher as it happens. I'd complained and assurances were made by the head teacher that she would look into it, but nothing changed. With the acute shortage of qualified teachers, schools could not afford to be picky about employees.

A bell rang and the staffroom filled up quickly. I approached one of the more curious women – they were all women – who was staring at me and told her I wanted to speak to people who had worked most closely with Janet Florin. 'She's missing,' I said, 'and her family are worried.'

'Oh, that's awful. You know she finished here?'

'Yes.'

She hesitated. 'Felicity is probably your best bet, Year 5.' She motioned to one of the oldest women there, who was dunking a tea bag in a mug marked World's Best Gran. 'And Lily, Janet's teaching assistant.' She gestured again.

I introduced myself to Felicity first and explained what I was there for.

'I didn't know her all that well,' Felicity said. 'She was only temporary.' She gave me a baleful look. 'Wish I was, sometimes.'

'Hard work?'

'It's all number crunching and ticking boxes nowadays. Somewhere like this, classes of thirty, maybe a third of them are statemented or have English as a second language, just getting through the day's a marathon. Not for the faint-hearted.'

'Was Janet faint-hearted?'

'Just fed up, I think.'

I cocked my head, invited her to continue.

'Her husband was out of work, I got the impression they were finding it harder to manage. She found this job pretty stressful. Still,' she paused, 'she didn't seem sorry to go when Julie came back from sick leave. Something she said...let me think...how she could always get work at short notice if a life of leisure didn't suit, but she'd had her fill of teaching.'

'A life of leisure?'

'I asked her but she got all coy, then.'

What could Janet have meant? She wasn't in any position to stop working indefinitely. A life of leisure? Had she secretly won the lottery, or something? And chosen to dump her family and spend it all on a new life for herself?

'Did she ever talk about moving away or leaving home – anything like that?'

Felicity shook her head.

Lily was a young Chinese woman with a Liverpudlian accent. She confirmed much of what Felicity had told me but expressed even greater shock that Janet had left home.

'Without the kids? That doesn't sound like Janet. I can't see her going off without her kids – she thought the world of them.' Trisha Marlowe had said the same. Had either of them known the real Janet Florin?

Janet's Monday evening yoga class was held in a church hall in Chorlton. The class started at 7 p.m. so I made sure I was there twenty minutes earlier in order to speak to the teacher beforehand. She arrived at 6.45; a small, wiry woman who drove a beat-up Citroën. I knew it was her when I saw her pulling mats and cushions from the boot. I got out of my car and followed her to the door. There was a beeping sound as she disabled the alarm. When I told her why I was there, she frowned. 'Janet Florin?'

I took out the photograph.

'Ah.' She recognised her. 'It's been a long time. She didn't re-enrol.'

'This term?'

'This year. We run from September. She never came back after the summer. There's always one or two who drop out.'

I stared at her. She walked on and I followed. She opened the large hall door and once inside began to lay out the mats.

'Do you remember whether Janet had friends at the class?'

She wrinkled her face, shook her head. 'Sorry, no.'

I'd run out of questions.

'You could try the other yoga classes in the area,' she suggested. 'Sometimes people switch to a different night, or fancy trying another type.'

But I knew it wasn't that. Janet had let the world believe she still came here every week. Nine months. Nine months of

Monday nights when she'd left home pretending to attend the evening class but going where? The odds that she'd had an affair were shortening. I rang Mark Florin and asked if I could call round and pick up the photocopies I'd asked for.

The place looked much the same but he looked worse. Bleary-eyed, unshaven, an angry rash on his neck.

He handed me the papers but didn't offer me a drink or even invite me to sit down. He didn't ask about progress either, which struck me as unusual. When I began to volunteer information, still wondering whether I should disclose the bogus night classes yet, he held up his meaty hands.

'I don't want to know,' he said baldly. 'I went to the police because I was worried. They'll do what they can and that's good enough for me. If Trisha wants to waste her money then good riddance. They've enough of it sloshing around anyway. Tell her all this. Until you've actually found Janet, there's nothing I want to hear.'

'And if I've any more questions?' Would he cooperate.

He exhaled and I caught the fruity blast of alcohol. 'There's only one question.' He spoke deliberately. 'Where's my bloody wife?'

I left him to it. Maybe his dismissal was just another reaction to the stress he was under but I wasn't going to hang around while he took it out on me.

In contrast, Trisha and Steve Marlowe welcomed me with open arms. They lived in Mossley, a village in the countryside beyond Ashton-under-Lyne. Ashton's one of the satellite towns that ring Manchester. It took me half an hour to drive there from Mark Florin's.

The house was newly built in pale, honey-coloured sandstone. It sat near the top of the hill and commanded a sweeping view of the valley. One storey high, it featured a curving wall of glass along the front, interrupted by stone pillars. In front of the window was a sunken garden. The gravel driveway led past this and around the side of the house to the back where the sloping roof was covered with solar panels.

Trisha came out to meet me, a lively red setter bounding around her.

'Sal, this is Hector, crazy dog. You found us all right?'

'Amazing house.'

'One of Steve's projects.' She led the way inside. 'It's being monitored as we speak – energy efficiency. Steve's in eco-tech – renewable energy for buildings.'

The huge open-plan room spanned the front of the house. It had wooden floors and ceiling and the walls were painted a soft cream colour. The place was divided into separate areas with furnishings and frosted glass screens. One of these was blurry with motion, I realised it was a water-feature, though the water flowing down it was inaudible to me. Perhaps that was intentional; the constant sound of running water might begin to grate. Along the back wall were several doors which led, I assumed, into the kitchen, bathroom and bedrooms.

A man sat at a workstation at the far end, some forty or fifty feet away. He rose and came towards us. He was tall, average build, dressed in chinos and an open necked shirt.

'Steve, this is Sal Kilkenny. Sal, can I get you a drink? Tea, coffee, water?'

'Coffee'd be great, thanks.'

'Come and sit down,' Steve invited me. He had short, pewter grey hair, a weathered complexion and pale grey eyes.

'Private Investigator,' he said, pulling the knees of his trousers up as he sat down. 'Don't think I've ever met one in the flesh. How did you get into that line? Were you with the police?'

I laughed. 'No. Job creation scheme.'

'They still have those?'

'This was a while back. Think they call it New Deal now.'

'So, what do you do, apart from missing persons?' He tilted his head in the direction Trisha had gone. 'Electronic surveillance? Spook stuff?'

'Would I tell you, if I did?'

He laughed then.

'No,' I carried on. 'Some places specialise in corporate accounts: fraud, industrial espionage, security. I prefer to work for individuals, mainly domestic enquiries.'

'Marital?'

'Can be, or other family matters, adoption tracing.' I thought of Bob Swithinbank and his desire to find Sandra.

Trisha emerged, carrying a tray laden with coffee and amaretto biscuits. The coffee smelt rich and spicy and my mouth watered. Once we all had our cups and I'd accepted and devoured two biscuits, I told them what I'd established so far about Janet. Of course, the biggest news was the phantom evening class.

'I think the obvious explanation is the most likely one,' I said.

'An affair?' Steve asked.

Trisha was combing her fingers through the short spiky hair

at the back of her ear. 'She'd have told me,' she insisted. 'She knew about us,' she reminded Steve, 'from the word go. Before anyone else. She always told me how things were going with Mark. Especially the bad times. We confided in each other completely.' She flung her hands up.

'The children?' I suggested. 'Perhaps leaving the children was something she couldn't share with anyone.'

'And you are their godmother, Trish,' Steve pointed out. 'So, now what?' He asked me. 'You think she's run off with this bloke?'

'Makes sense.'

'But you've no idea who he is?'

'No. Seems like she kept the whole thing secret from everyone.'

'Mark was right, then.' Trisha rubbed her fingers along the edge of the coffee table.

'Mark's not very happy about my enquiries. He says he'd rather leave it to the police.'

'But you'll carry on,' she asked, alarmed at the prospect of me not doing.

'If you want me to.'

'God, yes. I want to know why she's done this to us all. Those children...'

'And Mark,' Steve said archly.

There was a moment's tension then Trisha spoke. 'She should never have married him.'

I looked at her.

She took a breath. Pressed her fingertips against the tabletop, looking down as she spoke. 'He took her for granted. And once the children came along, she did everything. Oh, I know a lot of women do, but he never appreciated her. If she tried to talk about it, he'd storm out. He'd a chip on his shoulder the size of a…of a…something huge.'

Steve chuckled.

'You know what I mean,' she appealed to him.

He nodded.

'Chip about what?' I asked.

'You name it.' She gave a little shrug of impatience.

'Although, to be fair, the guy has lost his job,' Steve protested.

'He was just the same before, always something to complain about. It's so wearing,' Trisha said.

'What work was he doing?' I asked.

'Selling insurance,' she replied.

'And the interview he had in Liverpool?'

'It was in the same line, a bigger firm.' She clicked her fingers trying to summon the name. 'Glennisters Acorn. He didn't get it.'

'We consulted on their new-build,' Steve said. 'Place on the docks. Redevelopment.'

'You do the consultancy?' I asked him.

'Site research and development. It feeds into the feasibility studies.'

'It means he gets to travel here, there and everywhere and doesn't get stuck behind a desk,' Trisha teased him.

'Exactly,' he said.

'I still can't believe it,' Trisha brought us back to business, 'how could she?' Her face narrowed with anger. 'You've got to find this man; you've got to find them.'

* * *

The next morning, I settled with a flipchart and coloured pens to create an outline of Janet's timetable in the month leading up to her disappearance. Cross-referencing her address book with the itemised phone bill and then matching the credit card entries and bank statement with locations or types of purchase gave me a pattern to her movements. One thing was clear from the outset: the family were badly in debt. Their joint account was running an £8,000 overdraft, they'd a loan for another £10,000 and Janet owed £9,500 on her Visa. She only ever paid off the minimum amount. The couple were paying over £500 a month in interest alone, maybe more if Mark had his own credit cards as well.

The joint account spending was pretty much taken up with supermarket shops, petrol and direct debits. But when I charted the credit card, I saw that Janet had spent a lot of money on clothes in that last month, though not in the previous two. Buying from High Street stores like River Island, Next, Debenhams and La Senza; the lingerie outlet. Acquiring a new wardrobe for her new life? Or was she coping with the pressures of debt by grabbing some retail therapy? Were the clothes at her house? Mark had been uncertain about whether anything was missing – he thought not, only her handbag. But maybe Janet had put them in a case, a new one, that Mark hadn't known about? It would be helpful to have a good look around with Trisha – she had an eye for fashion and no doubt would be able to spot new items among her friend's outfits or gaps where clothes were missing. Something to tell us what she had worn that day, and whether her new items had been packed and taken. Would Mark oblige us?

Returning to the documents, I searched through for any clues to her movements on the Monday nights, when Janet swapped yoga for something clandestine. Some weeks, she withdrew cash on her card but there were no purchases from restaurants or hotels or anything that screamed illicit affair.

I took a break, drank some coffee with my feet up, gazing at the bright strip of sunlight that reached the narrow basement window in my office. There had been no word from Ramin so presumably no new sightings of Berfan. Rachel had thought it possible that Berfan had done a runner, to escape deportation. But if that was his intention, the scuffle at the casual labour pick-up point and the begging in town seemed reckless in the extreme. That sort of behaviour got him noticed; it didn't render him invisible. If we had no more news of Berfan I wasn't sure what more I could do.

Draining my cup, I tried to remember if there was enough fresh food in the house for tea. Would Ray have done any shopping? Not likely without a nudge. I'd barely seen him in the last couple of days. Was he particularly busy, or just giving me space? Or had his weekend break altered his feelings?

Just sleep with him – Diane's words. My stomach lurched as I thought about actually making a move. Where would we go? His room, my room? The phone rang and jerked me away from the speculation. For an insane moment, I expected Ray to be on the other end.

It was Bob Swithinbank, anxious for a response from his birth mother. 'Anything?'

'No.'

A pause.

'This is… I can't sleep,' he said. 'My guts are shot at. Can't you go see her?'

'Listen, she's probably still dealing with the shock. There's a risk that any other approach now will make it harder, put her under more pressure. People can retreat in that situation.' Take it slowly – that was my advice in all tracing investigations. Along with being realistic about outcomes. Of course that was hard – people couldn't help dreaming. For some, reunion really was a dream come true. For a handful, it was a bad dream and then there were those who found it a nightmare – torn apart when they were rejected all over again.

'I get you,' Bob said, 'but what if she's not got the letter, what if she's moved again or it got delivered wrong?'

'You need to give her time.'

He swore then apologised. 'I don't need an answer yet – I just need to know she actually got it. I've just got this feeling.'

'What?'

'I can't explain. That something's gone wrong. Some stupid sixth sense. Please. Just find out if she has it.'

I hesitated, I'd rather have waited as I'd already explained to him but at the end of the day, it was Bob's quest, his future in the balance.

'And if she has got it, we leave it at that for now? Agreed?'

'Yep.'

'OK, I'll do what I can.'

I couldn't ring Sandra Patefield. She wasn't listed in the phone book. Did she work? Would she be home during the day? Only one way to find out.

CHAPTER TEN

Wythenshawe was Manchester's garden city – that was the plan. In the 1920s, families from Hulme and Salford, from the worst of the teeming Victorian slum terraces, the places made infamous by Engels' writings, found themselves transported to houses with inside toilets, running water and gardens. The streets were broad and tree-lined. Unpaved at first and there were no amenities in place, but after the choking fog of the inner city, Wythenshawe was heaven. Sixty years on, the neighbourhood close to Manchester Airport was synonymous with deprivation and the crime that fed off it.

The large front garden at Sandra Patefield's corner semi was scattered with a motley assortment of ornaments and debris. Two garden gnomes, a waist-high Dutch windmill turning lazily in the wind, a stack of old bread-trays, a dead umbrella, assorted bits of metal, a plastic bird table and a stack of paving stones were the pieces I could identify. A cat lay draped across an old exhaust pipe, soaking up the sun. It raised its head as I walked up the path and struggled to open its eyes.

I rang the bell and heard it buzz inside, caught the sweet scent of wallflowers from the garden next door.

The woman who opened the door was heavily built and wore a navy tunic, a long skirt and a deep frown. She'd short, pine-coloured hair, dark at the roots, a full pink face and large, muddy blue eyes.

'Sandra Patefield?'

'Yeah,' she said shortly.

'I wrote to you last week – Sal Kilkenny. I wanted to check you got the letter.'

'You needn't bother. It's gone in the bin with the rest of them.'

Her hostility took me aback. Before I could say anything, she carried on. 'I've had it up to here with you lot and your bleedin' letters. I'll see you in court before I pay a penny.'

'There's no money involved.'

'Arrears.'

'No.' I was struggling to catch up.

'You from the council?'

'No, it's a private matter.'

'Our Susan?'

'No.'

Her frown was less hostile and more puzzled.

A couple of teenage lads passed slowly by, one had a Rottweiler puppy on a chain, the other pushed a skinny motorbike which made a hellish screeching sound as the wheels went round.

'Can I come in a minute and explain?'

'Yer not with the bailiffs?'

'No, really.'

She murmured assent and moved back into the house. 'Pull it hard,' she instructed me about the door, 'it sticks.'

The first door off the tiny vestibule was ajar –we went in there, the living room. The widescreen TV was on mute. A tabby cat lay on the sofa and beside it curled two kittens. One ginger, one grey. The ginger one stretched and yawned, flashing a bright pink tongue and tiny, needle teeth. The suite was dark brown and covered in cat hairs. The room was done up in mock-Tudor style with beams stuck to the ceiling and lumpy Artex painted white between them. The walls were deep red with baronial coats of arms stencilled here and there, the curtains were heavy stripes: green, maroon and cream. On the back wall hung a mirror framed between crossed swords and a huge photo portrait: a boy and a girl in school uniform, aged about ten or eleven. Bob's half-siblings? On the bulky sideboard below the mirror a clutch of birthday cards were displayed. Variations in pink. Sweet sixteen on several. Was this the Susan that Sandra had mentioned?

Sandra sat in the armchair furthest from the door and I sat down gently beside the cats.

'The letter...' I started.

'Be in the pile with that lot.' She jerked her head at a stack of mail on a table beside the telly.

'Can I?'

She nodded, adjusted her weight in the chair and stretched out her feet. One ankle was bandaged.

I went and sorted through. In among the circulars and official-looking envelopes, some marked urgent, I found the letter I'd sent, still sealed in its envelope.

'You haven't read it?'

'Nah.' She made an odd movement, her eyes dipping away, her hand covering her mouth.

'Would you like to?'

She kept her face turned away from me, her lips tightened. She shook her head. 'My glasses.'

In a rush, I understood. She couldn't read.

'What's it about anyway?'

I ran my finger along the flap and opened the envelope. I'd no intention of reading it out verbatim but the identifying dates were there for me to refer to.

The yawning kitten got to its feet and climbed the back of the sofa then ran along the edge to the end. It jumped the small gap across and into Sandra's lap. She rubbed its head.

'I'm a private detective. Some of my work involves tracing people.'

Her hand stilled.

'A man came to see me. He was born in February 1976, February 19th. He was adopted.'

'It's not me.' She stood suddenly, the ginger kitten clinging to her skirt for a moment before it tumbled to the floor. 'It's not me,' she said again. She was agitated; her hands flew to her face then she gripped them together in the middle of her chest. Her chin was wobbling with little shakes of her head. 'Some sort of mix-up.' She crossed to the door.

'He doesn't need an answer now,' I told her. 'He'd just like to talk – when you're ready. That's all. I know it's a big shock.'

'It's a big mistake, that's what it is.' She spoke bluntly but there was a tremor in her voice.

'I'll leave this,' I put the letter down on the sofa, 'my number's on there. Ring anytime. There's the number of an adoption counselling service too. They talk to birth parents a lot. They understand what it's like.'

She went ahead of me to the front door. She had to step outside to let me past. There the sun still bathed the cat on the exhaust pipe and the breeze still danced across the grass.

'He mustn't come here,' she said quickly.

I nodded. 'I'll tell him. He doesn't want to upset you. He's not going to barge in. He realises you've another life, now. But, please, think about it, about ringing me up. He just wants to talk, find out how you are.'

She gazed across the garden and beyond. I wondered what she saw. Herself as a pregnant teenager? The baby boy – newborn, feeding, crying? The building she stood in on the day she handed him over? Whatever it was, it wasn't the dozy cat, or the garden gnomes or the windmill circling languidly round and round.

At home, I sat outside to eat my lunch; nothing fancy, just a Cheddar cheese and salad sandwich and a banana.

The pond had settled and I could see through the water to the mud on the bottom. But the liner around the side walls looked horrible and plasticky. Hopefully with time it would grow a layer of green slime and when I'd got plants those would break it up a bit.

A sparrow came and alighted on one of the pebbles, looking round nervously before taking a drink from the water. Brilliant. I felt a surge of satisfaction.

Digger padded outside and whined at me hopefully. 'No can do,' I told him. 'Just eaten.' Ray took care of the dog but lately I'd let Digger accompany me on my sprints in the park.

I go to a weekly self-defence class in order to maintain the skills to protect myself if work gets dangerous. The moves I'd learnt there had saved my life not so long ago. I'd no interest in the grades and belts side of it all, just needed to be up to scratch with a few sure-fire tactics. Alongside that, being able to run reasonably fast is high on my list. And although I maintain a 'business not pleasure' attitude to fitness, I do get a buzz from sudden speed. There's something about the release of energy, the sensation of pelting along, arm and legs pumping, lungs sucking for air that takes me straight back to the gleeful chases and races of childhood. Running then went hand-in-hand with adventure: I was an Indian, a winged horse, a brave fugitive, a spirit, a cheetah. The same bubbles of excitement fizz in my blood when I dash across the park. They just don't show on the outside.

I locked the house up and went round the corner to my office. When I tried Bob's number, I couldn't get through. His itinerary meant that they were en route from Germany to Bosnia. They could be in the air. Even on the ground there were pockets of lousy reception, he'd warned me. I'd try later.

Should I have dug my heels in and refused to follow up on Sandra so soon? She'd panicked as I'd feared but on the other hand there had been some foundation to Bob's sixth sense that the woman might not have got the letter. Not having read it, she knew nothing of his quest until I intervened. And yes, although she panicked and scrabbled to deny his existence, her parting words, *he mustn't come here,* acknowledged the truth. Now she needed time to mull over the prospect of contact with him.

I returned to Janet's case. There were four numbers listed on the itemised phone bill that didn't match the contacts I found in her address book. I got through to all of them: a local cinema, a woman who we worked out was the mother of a school friend of Jacob Florin (Janet had rung to RSVP a birthday invite), a pizza delivery place and Network Rail enquiries. My ears pricked up at this last one. Janet hadn't driven away in a car – so had she gone by train?

I studied the credit card details again. Nothing paid to Network Rail, Virgin Trains or any other carrier. Janet's last credit card purchase had been on the Saturday before her disappearance. Since then nothing. I checked the joint current account printout. Just a couple of modest withdrawals from the bank near their house in the ensuing days.

What on earth was she living on? Was she living?

The thought brought me out of my chair. My guts cramped. Ridiculous. You can't prove a negative. No spending doesn't equal – what? Suicide, accident, murder? Get a grip, I told myself. There was no point in getting bound up in fantastic speculation.

I stretched my arms, rotated my head, trying to clear my mind. Then I sat down again and went back to meticulous checking and cross-referencing. When I'd gone as far as possible, I listed the fragments of information from everyone who'd spoken to me.

Consciously relaxing, I let my mind roam around, picking up one phrase or notion, then another. *She was more excited than happy*, from the hairdresser, *she didn't make her next appointment. A life of leisure...asked her what she meant and she went all coy*, from the teacher Felicity. *She was more interested in sex*, Mark's gruff revelation.

What was Janet's story? What account covered the facts so far? I drew a line down the length of a new piece of paper. On one side, I noted everything that supported the possibility that

Janet had run off with someone, leaving her husband and children; on the other anything that contradicted that. The contradictions included lots of people claiming she'd never leave her kids, the fact that Janet hadn't taken her address book, her passport or essential items like her birth certificate. She hadn't told Mark or Trisha what she was planning, nor left a note trying to explain. If she was the good mother people painted her yet she'd decided to leave home wasn't doing it this way – not turning up at school, leaving without a word – the most cruel and frightening way to behave?

That day Mark had gone to his interview, hopeful perhaps about a new opportunity in Liverpool. Something niggled at me. I fished out the bank statements for their joint account. Thursday 10th. Mark had got petrol. I had assumed it was him but could that have been Janet? Driving away with her lover and using her bankcard, perhaps realising then that it would leave an unwelcome trail and deciding not to use it anymore.

I looked the location up on the Internet. Got one hit – a service station some forty-five miles north-east of Manchester, in Yorkshire. And Mark Florin had been nowhere near, he'd been in an interview most of the day. He'd set off early in the morning to beat the rush hour and was still on the journey home when school rang his mobile to tell him the children hadn't been collected. It must be Janet! A thrill tickled the pulse in my wrists. I needed more to confirm it though. The easiest way would be ruling Mark out. *Most of the day*, was too vague. When had he left Liverpool?

His answerphone was on when I tried him. I felt a sense of relief. He might well have told me where to stuff my questions if our last encounter was anything to go by. However, Trisha had mentioned the firm Mark had applied to, it was there in my notes. Directory enquiries offered to connect me to Glennisters Acorn in Liverpool. Now that data protection is on everyone's tick-lists, I wasn't about to ask directly what time an individual called Mark Florin had left them. As the automated voice told me how much I was being charged for the service, I was spinning alternative undercover guises in my mind. 'Hello,' I practised, 'I'm doing some research into patterns of recruitment in Merseyside, I wonder whether you could answer a few simple questions?'

'Hello, Glennisters Acorn.'

'Hello, could you put me through to Human Resources or Recruitment?'

'Sorry, they're not based here. You need our Milton Keynes branch.'

'Oh, erm, is there someone there I could speak to about the interviews you held in June?'

'We haven't had any interviews.'

'June 10th.'

'No. Not since March. They only hold them every six months. The next ones will be September.'

'Are you sure?'

'Absolutely.'

'Thank you.' My mouth went dry and heat flared across my skin. I put the phone down. If Mark hadn't been in Liverpool being interviewed, where had he been? In Yorkshire? Why the pretence? Was that the reason for his antagonism? Because he didn't want anyone looking too closely into his wife's sudden disappearance? Because of what they might find? Had he really spoken to the police, or just told us all that? Had Trisha actually spoken to the police or just Mark? Questions sprouted and multiplied. I didn't like where this was heading – not one little bit. I'd a sickening sensation in the pit of my stomach and the urge to distance myself from the phone, from the office, from the case. Not an option. But now what the hell was I going to do?

CHAPTER ELEVEN

I ran. Not away – just around the corner to the park. I couldn't sit still, and my mind was ricocheting around like a trapped bird. The run gave rhythm to my thoughts. A swim would have done the same job but taken three times as long.

What had I got at the end of the day? One lie, that's all. One lie. One lie didn't equal foul play. Perhaps Mark Florin had talked up the interview, pretending it was for a bigger firm. Perhaps the interview had been with a similar-sounding company or a subsidiary.

Obviously, I had to ask him for an explanation but I realised he'd be just as likely to show me the door as give me an answer. As I needed other information about Janet, about her clothes and personal belongings, it made sense to get hold of that first before challenging him.

After twenty minutes pounding round the perimeter paths I'd burnt off some of the adrenalin, calmed down and decided on my next step.

Trisha was godmother to his children, so I hoped Mark would be obliging if the request to look through Janet's things came from her. She was happy to ask and rang me back within minutes. We could call at the Florins' the following morning.

Mark had an appointment at the job centre but if we got there for 10.30 he'd let us in on his way out. I didn't mention the bogus interview to Trisha – it wasn't appropriate until I'd verified the facts. But it festered in my mind like a splash of acid, sharp and caustic.

That evening Bob Swithinbank called me.

'Sandra got the letter,' I told him, 'but it's been a real shock. You need to give her some time.'

'Did you see her?' His voice went squeaky with excitement.

'Yes, briefly. It looks like she has two other children, in their teens, I think. A boy and a girl.'

'Oh, wow. A brother and a sister.'

'You were an only child, growing up?'

'That's right. Oh, man,' he said still bowled over by the news.

'When do you get back?'

'Sunday, late.'

'Come round here on Monday and I can bring you up to date.'

'Cool. So, I was just being neurotic,' he giggled, 'thinking she'd not got the letter.'

'No, not exactly. She hadn't looked at the letter – she assumed it was from the council until I called.' When I saw Bob I would explain about Sandra's reading difficulty. It felt like delicate information not something to throw into a quick phone call.

He couldn't resist another question. 'What's she like?'

How do you answer that? A person asking what their birth mother is like, their head full of hopes and fantasies. It wasn't fair to share my first impressions; we'd got off on the wrong foot and I'd dropped a bombshell into her life. I settled for something objective.

'She's big, like you.'

He laughed. 'Fat you mean? Thank God for that – it'd have been weird, you know, if she was stick thin.' He exhaled loudly. 'It's brilliant you know, bloody brilliant – she's there. She's really there. Thanks, you know. A lot, like, really.' He was increasingly inarticulate. But his relief and excitement sang like a bell.

The sun was still shining, the patio shimmering in the heat and we ate tea outside. Ray had done pesto and pasta and a tomato salad. He helped Maddie and Tom make boats out of wood off-cuts and they floated them on the pond. When Digger got thirsty he drank from the water.

'Oy,' I remonstrated, nudging the dog aside with my foot. 'I didn't make it for you.'

'It's coming on,' Ray said.

'Needs plants.' I checked my watch. 'I could go now.'

'You could,' a smile tugged at his mouth, 'or you could stay here and soak up the sun.' He stroked his own chest, his hand tanned against the white cotton T-shirt.

'I might get burnt.' I stared at his lips, gazed at his eyes. Standing up, my legs felt shaky.

''Spose you might,' he teased.

'Maddie, Tom, you want to come to the garden centre?'

They did.

* * *

Water plants were pricey so I limited myself to some Elodea to oxygenate the water and spiky deep green rushes with little bands of black around the reeds. Maddie and Tom clamoured for ornaments, a shipwreck, a skull, a giant pink shell. No way. My pond was going to be a kitsch-free zone. If they wanted the knick-knacks for their room... After some debate, they each chose a plant to bring home. Tom plumped for a prickly pear cactus, 'like cowboys have', and Maddie picked a cherry tomato plant. She promised to share her crop with the rest of us.

Ray was out for the evening. Quiz night, sacrosanct. They win quite regularly. Once the children were asleep, I surfed the channels for a while then gave up and turned to my book. My mind kept drifting back to Ray, to the way he'd stroked his chest, like a cat preening or a dog stretching. His eyes narrowing against the sunlight. Ray flirting with me and the tingle thrilling through me, gripping the base of my neck, lapping at the back of my knees, the roof of my mouth. I dreamt about him that night. Raunchy. That's all I'm saying.

Ramin rang me early on Wednesday. He'd not made any progress and didn't know what to do next.

'The argument Berfan had, when he was in the line for work,' I said.

'Yes?'

'Try and find out who he spoke to. What was behind the fight.'

'It's too late now,' Ramin said, 'they meet at six o'clock.'

'OK. Well, we could go in the morning but before that ask the man who told us about it, the one at the Welcome Centre, if he knows who the guy was. I'll check with the police and hospitals again.'

Greater Manchester Police headquarters confirmed that Berfan had not been arrested or charged and was not in custody. And he wasn't a patient with the NHS either.

Trisha's Rover was already outside the Florins' house when I got there. She let me in. 'Mark's just left. You want to start with her clothes?'

'Yes.'

In the master bedroom, the alcoves either side of the old chimney breast had been fitted out as wardrobes. Trisha rifled through the skirts, blouses and dresses that were hanging up and the jumpers and fleeces on the shelves.

'Anything obviously missing?'

'She had a trouser suit, in linen, a deep rose colour, I can't see that. But that's the only thing.'

'Anything here strike you as new? Something you've not seen Janet wear before?'

Trisha looked puzzled.

'She'd been shopping recently. I'm wondering whether she took her new stuff with her.'

Trisha looked again and came up with a dress, a delicate blouse and a long ruffled skirt that she didn't remember. When I asked her to check the shoes she pointed out some green sling-backs that were new. The labels on all these items corresponded to stores on the credit card statement.

'Her underwear will be here,' I guessed, opening the top of the chest of drawers. There's something seedy about picking through a woman's bras and knickers but I'd good reason to do so. No shiny new undies from La Senza as far as I could see. Was she wearing them? Maybe they'd been bought as a gift for someone else.

What our search did establish, was that Janet had taken next to nothing clothes-wise. Not even her recent purchases. Trisha realised that too. 'If you're running off with somebody, surely you'd pack a bag.' Her eyes registered dismay.

A feeling matched by the cold swirl in my stomach. Before she could elaborate on her fears, I played devil's advocate. 'Maybe there is no secret lover, she just upped and went. On her own, spur of the moment. Something got to her. She intends to come back.'

OK, it sounded a bit unlikely but all we had was conjecture and I needed more time, more facts in hand before I entertained other possibilities out loud.

'Why couldn't she tell me?'

'You might have talked her out of it.'

Downstairs, we looked at the coats hanging by the back door and again Trisha couldn't see anything gone. 'Though if she had her trouser suit on, that's enough this time of year.'

I thought about the last petrol purchase on the joint account. 'Do you know Grassington, in Yorkshire?'

'I know of it. Been there once, I think. Why?'

'Any connection to Mark or Janet?'

She wrinkled her nose, thought about it. 'No. Why?'

'Something on the bank statement, that's all.'

We heard Mark's key in the door and we both jumped as though caught out. 'I'd like to keep things between us, for now,' I told her, hoping she wouldn't quibble about it.

She hesitated before giving a quick nod.

Mark was shrugging off his jacket as we came into the hall.

'Mark,' she said, 'I was wondering if Isobel and Jacob would like to come to us for the weekend.'

'I can ask them.'

'Give you a break.'

He looked away sharply and I saw her kindness had caught him unawares. He coughed. 'I'll give you a ring.'

The air was hot with tension as we filed past him to the door.

'Can I ask you a question?' I said.

'You can ask.'

'Were you in Grassington anytime on the 10th?'

'Grassington?' He frowned.

'In Yorkshire.'

'I know where Grassington is. I was in Liverpool all day.' He looked at me angrily, his neck flushed, jaw set.

'Did Janet know anyone there?'

'No. Why?'

I hesitated.

'Just some lead you're following, is it?' he said. 'Well, I can't help you.'

Or you won't, I thought.

'Mark,' Trisha protested gently at his tone.

'It's all right,' I said.

'You've no idea,' he said to Trisha.

'About what?' She sounded stung.

He shook his head, defeated now, and waved us away.

* * *

We stood outside beside her car. 'He won't let me help,' she complained. 'He's acting as if he's the only one who cares. She's my best friend, damn it. And those children are my...' Her voice trembled, her eyes brimmed.

'Come back for coffee,' I suggested. 'There's a few more things I'd like to hear about.'

Settled in my office, Trisha answered my question about the Florins' finances as best she could.

'Janet didn't tell me much, just that things were a bit tight.'

'They owe at least thirty thousand pounds.'

Trisha didn't seem fazed by this. The Marlowes were much better off so thirty grand wouldn't be the same burden to them. I put it in context. 'Mark's not bringing anything in, well, only what he gets from registering unemployed. Jobseeker's Allowance is peanuts. The debt must be more than their annual income.'

Trisha finally baulked at that, her mouth rounding in surprise.

'There were tensions in the relationship,' I stated. 'And that sort of debt brings pressures of its own. How would Janet react to the stressful situation?'

'She'd make the best of it. She felt she owed it to the children.' She paused, took a breath. Her dark brown eyes moved to the left as she fished for the memory. 'There was a time when Isobel was tiny and Janet was finding it hard to manage. Mark was working then, overtime as well, so she was on her own a lot. Isobel was a bad sleeper and she had Jacob on top of that. Janet would ring me in tears, she was shattered. I persuaded her to explain to Mark how it was. Thinking that he could give her a bit of support. It was disastrous; he took it as criticism and got all huffy about how he was slaving away and wasn't appreciated.' Trisha brushed back her spiky fringe. 'If he'd just given her a hug, said he understood... Anyway that's the only time I remember her having serious doubts about the marriage, about whether it had been a mistake. But she got through it and after that she just got on with things. Knuckled down. I'd have been long gone.' She gave a brittle laugh.

'What about Mark? I'm certainly not seeing the best of him. How important was the marriage to him?'

'It's all he's got,' she said directly. 'That house, Janet, the kids – that's his life.'

And if someone threatened that – if there was a lover? 'Did they ever fight, ever any violence?'

'No.' She looked at me. She blinked, worked her lips. 'It's been two weeks.'

I nodded.

'Can't we go back to the police? She hasn't used her phone. She hasn't spent any money.' Trisha's voice was tight with anxiety.

'You both saw the police? You and Mark?'

'Yes.'

So the official wheels had been set in motion, Mark hadn't been bluffing about notifying the authorities.

'You can try. But I doubt that you'd get a different response.'

'What will you do next?'

'Janet may have been in Grassington. I'm going up there – see if I can pick up her trail.'

'You asked Mark about it.'

'Either of them could have used the card.'

'He was in Liverpool though.' Half a question, half a statement.

'I have to verify everything,' I said evading her actual query. I knew Mark was lying about his whereabouts but, if he did have anything to do with Janet going missing, he wasn't covering his tracks particularly well. He'd blithely handed over the financial documents I'd wanted. Did that mean the Grassington purchase was Janet's? If Mark had been there, why give me the evidence? Because of a subconscious desire to be found out? Or because he was arrogant and didn't think he could be caught?

CHAPTER TWELVE

That afternoon, as promised, I went with Diane to hospital. Christie's is a stone's throw from my house and a short bus ride from Diane's – she lives up in Rusholme. She came round to mine first. I smiled when I first saw her. She'd had her hair done for the occasion: extensions that must have cost a fortune and her own hair dyed to match, a rich dark chocolate colour.

'Make the most of it while I've got it,' she replied when I admired the look.

'You always do,' I told her. She loved messing with her hair.

'Just think of all those wigs,' she grinned. 'Next stop Flava.' She referred to the shop in town that sported a cornucopia of hats and wigs and accessories. I knew about it because I'd once bought something for a fancy-dress party there. Diane, however, was already a regular customer.

The sky was a sullen oyster shade and drizzled fine rain as we walked over to the hospital. A clutch of nurses stood puffing on cigarettes rather lowering the aesthetic of the smart glass-canopied entrance. We found our way to the waiting area for the consultant, Mr Stefanos. The place had a relentlessly cheery atmosphere with staff joshing each other, vases of flowers and lots of pictures on the freshly painted cream walls. I was glad it wasn't gloomy and shabby.

'Do you want me to come in with you?' I asked her.

'Yeah.'

'Fine.'

'Needs a bigger space,' Diane nodded at a seascape in thick acrylic, ever the artist.

'I don't like that one,' I muttered, tipping my head towards another painting. A portrayal of two women, it had an airbrushed, pastel quality that reminded me of bland greetings cards with appalling sugary verses inside. It was the sort of picture that people put up in dentist's waiting rooms or B&Bs solely because it's so bland it won't offend anybody.

We didn't have long to wait before a nurse called Diane's name. Mr Stefanos was a small, round, hairy man with a deeply scored forehead and a sombre, accented voice. He shook hands with both of us, gave us seats, established which of us was Diane and set to work.

Slowly and methodically, he explained that the needle biopsy they had taken had established a malignant growth but that the tumour was very small. My stomach contracted at the word malignant. Diane gave a jerky nod, this much she already knew.

'Everything indicates that this is the primary site of the cancer and it's at an early stage. There are no certainties in oncology but we have a wealth of experience to draw on and treatment improves every month. With an early stage presentation like this you can consider two types of surgery.' He used his fingers, which were covered in black hairs like werewolf gloves, to count them. 'A lumpectomy followed by radiotherapy, where we remove the tumour and use radiation therapy to reduce the risk of cancer returning to that area. Or a mastectomy, where we remove the whole breast, and where you are unlikely to also need radiotherapy. This is a more radical option, though breast reconstruction is available. Both these options give comparable results. It comes down to personal choice. With a lumpectomy, some surrounding tissue will be taken as well. If cancer cells are present there, then more surgery will be recommended, possibly a mastectomy.'

Sudden tears stung my eyes as I recognised the challenge Diane faced. The thought of her losing a breast seemed obscene. Big, busty Diane, who flaunted her chest with pride.

I tuned back into Mr Stefanos who was explaining about a cancer nurse who would be available to answer questions at any time and telling us about a fact pack the hospital gave out.

'And chemotherapy?' Diane asked.

'Chemotherapy is used to prevent re-occurrence. The drugs used can be given in many different combinations and they have different side effects. Depending on the nature of your cancer, lifestyle considerations, family history and so on you would choose a combination that most suits your particular situation.'

Diane asked him what option he would recommend.

His frown deepened. 'We've found the most successful outcomes are those where the patient feels she is making an informed choice.'

'What gives me the best chance?'

'Statistics in a case like yours are comparable. Mastectomy is reassuring for some women because it is radical. But it brings other elements into play: psychological, emotional. I want you to read the information, talk to the nurse if there's anything you don't understand and come back next Friday. The two options I've outlined each have an excellent chance of helping you. We've caught the cancer early, you're relatively young, but only you can make the best choice for yourself.'

'Oh, Sal,' Diane said later after she'd come out clutching the information pack. 'I don't want a bloody choice; I want them to tell me what's best.'

'I don't think he's being awkward – let's read the stuff.'

We went back to mine and had coffee and biscuits. Took turns browsing through each leaflet and FAQ sheet.

'What would you do?' She pulled the extensions back from her face, bunched them up like a ponytail.

'I knew you were going to ask me that.'

'Well?'

'Least intervention, I guess. I'd want to keep my breast.'

'And the risk of it returning?'

'All this,' I waved a leaflet, 'says it's about the same. So did Mr Stefanos.'

'They reckon the chemo's worse than the surgery or the radiotherapy.'

'Put you off your food for a bit.'

She kicked out at me.

'If it's all so similar then why go not go for the smallest op?' I asked.

She nodded. 'I suppose some women feel easier if they get rid. Especially if it's in the family.'

'Your mum didn't have cancer?'

'No, but my gran did and one of my aunties. Right.' She stood and stretched. 'I've work to do, expect you have too.'

'Yep. Give me a ring.'

We hugged.

When she'd gone and I'd closed the door, a rush of grief made me catch my breath. You'd better be all right, I thought sternly, you'd better bloody be all right.

At half past five the following morning, I picked Ramin up. The fresh feel to the day redeemed the shock of such an early start. There was a clarity to the light, moisture from the morning dew darkened the brick and stone and shone on trees and grass. Swifts and seagulls wheeled and dipped above and there was little traffic to drown out their cries.

Ramin was at the door before I had chance to get out of the car. He climbed in and greeted me.

'I know the man to see,' he said. 'He is Kurdish.'

'Are they all Kurdish?'

'Some Polish too, some Iranian, Somali.'

He directed me to a brownfield site near the motorway in Salford. When we arrived, men were standing in scattered groups. Many of them were smoking. One group were kicking a coke can about. They all paused and looked our way, only relaxing when Ramin got out of my car.

'Is he here?' I asked Ramin.

'Yes, at the end – in the green top.'

I saw the man. Similar in height and build to Ramin but with a beard. He stilled as we approached. Perhaps he thought Ramin meant trouble – payback for the fight with Berfan.

Ramin said something in Kurdish and the man replied. I saw his teeth glinted with gold fillings. Ramin asked something else and the guy answered with a reluctant mumble. Whatever he said provoked a reaction, both in Ramin, who tensed and glowered, and in the nearby onlookers who shuffled, avoiding eye contact with anyone.

'What's he saying?'

Ramin didn't answer me but spoke to the man, anger edging his voice. The man jerked his chin up in response and raised his tone. I caught the word Berfan once and the man waved his arms in some sort of pantomime. Someone nearby sniggered. Ramin swore – I didn't need a translator to get that – and strode off back to the car.

'What is it?' I asked him as I opened the doors and we climbed in. 'What did he say?'

Ramin put his head back, stared up at the roof. 'He say Berfan is crazy.'

'Crazy?'

'He say Berfan is talking…all things… *I am the chosen one, the…*' Ramin shook his head with frustration. 'What is the man who put shoes on the horse?'

'Blacksmith,' I supplied.

Ramin turned to me. 'Berfan say he is the blacksmith bringing holy fire.'

'What does that mean?'

'It is a story – from home.'

He glanced at me, shame in his eyes.

'Could he be ill – like that?'

'My brother is not crazy,' Ramin shouted, his face reddening.

There was a silence.

A minibus pulled into the site and the waiting men turned. I saw one or two straighten up, standing taller.

'We better go,' said Ramin. He jerked his head towards the minibus. 'They don't like people to watch.'

As we drove back, the city was waking up. Buses and cars now filled the streets. Motorbikes and cyclists wove among them. The motorway slip road was backed up with traffic. Drivers beginning the daily commute to Leeds or Liverpool or even further afield. Thank God I didn't have to do that to make a living; three hours a day just getting there and back with all the tension of modern driving.

By the time we reached Ramin's place, I'd worked out what I wanted to say. I turned off the engine and turned to him. 'It's something we need to consider. There are mental health units attached to the hospitals. I only checked general admissions. General hospitals.'

'He's not crazy,' he repeated.

'How do you know?'

He said nothing.

'I think I should make some calls.'

Had Ramin's reaction something to do with attitudes to mental illness in his culture? Or was he simply denying something he feared, as many of us might?

'You still want to find him?'

He nodded his head. He looked worn out and I wished I could reassure him somehow. We said goodbye. He walked back towards the little house with its narrow windows and bristling security.

CHAPTER THIRTEEN

I called Rachel, the social worker who'd introduced me to Ramin, from my office. I wanted to check with her the best way of covering mental health units in the area. I knew provision was in a state of flux as many residential facilities were re-locating to the large Wythenshawe hospital site. There had been lots of articles in the local press and angry letters from patients about it. If Berfan had been admitted to a psychiatric unit, would the places I'd already rung have that information?

'Luck of the draw,' Rachel said. 'I can check if you like, got the numbers to hand. And my boss is out at a meeting.'

'That'd be brilliant. Rachel, is there a stigma around mental illness in Iran?' I recalled a documentary on television some years ago which exposed attitudes to the mentally ill and disabled in Greece. Feared and excluded, the people had been dumped on an island in barbaric conditions and suffered terrible abuse.

'More than here, you mean? Don't think so. Hey—' her tone shifted, 'I heard about Diane. That's awful.'

'Yeah.'

'How's she coping?'

'OK. I don't know. It's all very new. But they've caught it early.'

'Give her my love,' Rachel said. 'My mum had it, and she beat it. People do.'

'Yeah.'

I felt wobbly again. All those women out there who'd battled with this, all their kids and parents and husbands. Every time someone talked about it, it was as if my perspective jumped; someone tilting the kaleidoscope or a camera zooming out, showing what really mattered.

After a coffee, I pulled out the Janet Florin file and used Google to research the petrol station in Yorkshire and plan my visit. By the end of the session, I'd downloaded maps of the area and a list of B&Bs and hotels, got the address of the filling station and printed out a route. The Yorkshire Dales are popular with tourists, especially walkers, as the Pennine hills offer breathtaking vistas and challenging climbs. The three peaks is a famous one, a day-long marathon that takes in the heights of a trio of mountains: Pen-y-ghent, Whernside and Ingleborough.

I rang Trisha and asked if she had any photos of Janet with the family. Although I already had one of Janet on her own, I wanted a picture with Mark in. He had repeated his lie about Liverpool to me. Maybe he had been travelling with Janet that day. And returned home without her.

'I've one of the four of them at Jacob's last birthday. It's digital. I can email it to you?'

'Excellent.'

It was a reasonable snapshot: Janet and Mark, she slender, her light brown hair brushing her shoulders, he blocky and dark-haired, standing together behind Jacob and Isobel who

were admiring a Shrek cake. All smiling for the camera. I
hadn't seen Mark smile since we'd met. It improved his image
no end.

Walking the kids home from school, I watched Tom run, then
stop and adopt a martial arts pose and launch an attack at his
imagined foe. The trees were heavy with foliage, the early
summer growth thriving in the mix of sun and rain that we'd
had. The weeds were thriving too and fluffy seeds from the
first dandelion clocks floated in the air.

Maddie flummoxed me by asking what cancer was.

'It's a disease, an illness.'

'Can you catch it?'

'No. Where did you hear about it?'

'This boy's got it, in Year 6.'

'Is he going to die?' asked Tom who had run back and
caught the conversation.

'A lot of people get better,' I told them. 'They have medicine
or an operation.'

'He's bald,' said Maddie.

'Yes, that's a side effect of the tablets. Diane's got cancer.'

'Will she go bald,' Tom asked, 'or is it just boys?'

'She might.'

'What's a side effect?' Maddie asked.

By the time I'd explained that one, they'd lost interest and
the topic changed to potential names for potential frogs in our
new pond. Maddie settled on Charlie for a boy frog and
Croakette for a girl (despite my warning that frogs were very
difficult to sex) and Tom went for Bouncer and Miss
Terminator.

Ray had put a vegetable casserole together so I just had to turn the oven on when we got back. It was all ready when he came home from work. The kids liked the juice but not the 'lumps' so they dipped their garlic bread in that and had cubes of cheese on sticks – which as everybody knows tastes completely different to cheese in any other shape.

'You in tonight?' Ray asked. I felt him stroke my foot with his.

'Yes.'

'I've got a DVD if you fancy.' Brown eyes bright. Another stroke.

I grinned and winked. Footsie at the tea table. I was an adolescent again. 'Stop it,' I mouthed at him.

He frowned. 'What?'

Another brush from his foot. I bent down and peered under the table. There lay Digger, his tail slowly beating to and fro with simple canine pleasure. Footsie! My cheeks suddenly aglow, I emerged and busied myself clearing the plates.

Later, with the kids in bed and the DVD starting, Ray handed me a glass of wine and filled his own. I took a mouthful, then another. He sat beside me and I could feel the hairs on my scalp and my arms lift and prickle. He took a drink. I watched him swallow, his eyes drifting shut for a moment, the long lashes spilling shadows onto his tan skin, his Adam's apple bobbing. He looked at me and smiled. I gazed at his teeth then felt a lurch of self-consciousness. I drank some more. Studying the glass, the depth of colour in the pinot noir.

'Hey.' He spoke softly, his voice husky. I turned to him.

He reached out a hand, stroked a strand of hair back from

my face and cupped his palm against my cheek. The skin on
his hand was slightly rough, testament to his carpentry. I
wanted that hand, those hands, all over me; stroking the
length of my back and my calves, my neck and my hips.

Parting my lips, I leant forward, into him. The kiss was soft
and slow and warm. It started a slow burn that travelled to
my breasts and my belly and my sex. I gave a murmur and
Ray responded, one hand moving down my back, the other
trailing down my neck and on to brush my breast.

I pulled away. Dizzy. Sherbet in my veins.

'Sal?' Disappointment flooded his eyes, his cheeks were
darker with excitement, his breath irregular.

'Let's go upstairs,' I said. I'd changed my sheets, in case,
tidied up, put the small lamp on, a bunch of freesia to perfume
the air. All the while telling myself that these actions didn't
commit me to anything. As if Ray hadn't seen my room in
every state of mess.

He closed his eyes and slowly opened them again.

Like fugitives, we tiptoed upstairs carrying the wine and
our glasses. Digger made a half-hearted attempt to follow but
Ray froze him with a gesture.

I filled our glasses and set them on the chest of drawers. We
kissed again. I noticed the contrast of his smooth, soft lips with
the texture of his moustache. He pulled me closer and I could
feel the shape of him against me. I kissed him more urgently, the
desire sparking everywhere from my scalp to my toes.

Ray stepped back and began to undress me, pulling off my
T-shirt and strap-top, then touching me, kissing again. I
wanted to be naked, both of us naked. Moving away, I took
off my pants and briefs. The air was slightly cool on my skin

and when he touched me, his hands were hot and dry and hungry. I pulled at his T-shirt and tugged it off. Then the rest.

We stood together, skin to skin. My fingertips were tingling, my lips moist and swollen. He kissed my mouth, my throat, my shoulder. I ran my hands down his shoulder blades, down to his buttocks. He sighed and I felt a swoon of lust.

I led him to my bed.

I woke him at 1.30. We'd drifted off some time before. He lay on his back, snoring lightly, his leg lay across mine, which had gone numb.

He murmured a greedy sound and tried to kiss me, his eyes lidded with sleep.

'You should go to your room. I don't want Maddie or Tom coming in.'

'You think?'

'I do.'

''K,' he said lazily, then dived at me for a kiss.

He made me giggle but that soon stopped as my lips responded and my body became flushed with heat again.

'No,' I pulled away, 'I've an early start.'

He nodded. Propped up on one elbow, he looked at me. A loving look, his mouth curved with a gentle smile, his eyes limpid. He bent and kissed me, tender, and broke off just as I began to grow giddy. He gathered up his clothes and paused at the door.

'*Arriverderchi*,' he said, fluttering his eyelashes. For all the world a Latin gigolo.

I burst out laughing, wriggled my fingers at him, saying goodnight.

CHAPTER FOURTEEN

The Pennine mountain range forms the backbone of England and divides the counties of Lancashire in the west (where Manchester was before they invented Greater Manchester) from Yorkshire in the east. The M62 motorway crosses the hills and to get onto that I had to drive to Stockport and take the M60 near the landmark glass pyramid building.

I'd hoped to beat the rush hour but by eight o' clock it was already in full swing and the leg from home in Withington to the start of the ring road took three times as long as usual.

The western spur of the M60 was fairly recent, the regimented sticks supporting saplings were all too visible along the banks. Some bozo had designed a junction where traffic joined the motorway on the right – straight into the fast lane. And they'd actually gone ahead and built it. I always hold my breath going past there, and resist the temptation to close my eyes as well.

Some sections are prone to flooding too, another triumph of twenty-first-century design, but the dry weather overnight meant the area was clear.

Traffic doubled once I reached the M62. Lorry land, with articulated trucks travelling the breadth of the country from ports on the west like Holyhead and Liverpool over to Hull on the eastern seaboard. I saw one lorry from Norway, another from Spain and even one thundering past from South Africa. The road runs through high moorland climbing into Yorkshire and, at the summit, a sign boasts the highest motorway in England, 1221 feet. It's a stunning landscape but I had to concentrate on the traffic, only occasionally noticing the purple shadows of clouds racing over the gold and green moorland. The sweep of sky and land and fall of the valleys gave me that top of the world sensation.

An hour later, I reached the bypass near Skipton, the town that proclaims itself the gateway to the Dales. As I drove on, the mill towns that embroidered the valleys nearer to the motorway were left behind, replaced by small country villages and market towns, all built in the light grey limestone of the area. The day was bright and matched my mood. Memories from the night before came back to me sporadically, little moments to savour. Any consideration about whether I'd done the right thing in letting things develop with Ray, was shoved aside by the sheer pleasure of the experience. I felt energised. Diane would be delighted. I realised that what was happening to Diane probably had some bearing on my actions. The threat of illness, the fear of death, spurring a desire for connection. Sex as a way of affirming life. Did it matter? No.

The smaller roads I took wove between dry-stone walls. Windswept hawthorns with gnarled limbs showed which way the wind blew. Lambs, their tails shivering like carnival garlands, bounced about in the fields while the sheep grazed. Large, black crows were everywhere and although the hills were bare of trees, down in the pastures an ancient elm or oak or a small copse of trees stood in many a corner or along the run of the dry-stone walls.

With the window open, I could smell the bitter grassy scent and now and then caught snatches of the high, stinky smell of the elderflower which bloomed here later than in the milder Manchester climate.

The petrol station I wanted was just outside Grassington village. Six pumps and a forecourt shop. As I'd hoped, there were security cameras mounted on the corners of the shop roof.

The young woman at the till had long ginger hair, a lip ring and lumpy mascara caking her lashes like black sugar.

'Hello,' I said. 'I'm a private detective.'

She grinned and cracked her gum. 'This a wind-up?'

'No, really.' I showed her my card.

'You can get them done at the station,' she said, 'anyone can do one. Or on the computer.'

'I'm the real thing, though. And I'm trying to find a missing person. Either she, or her husband, bought petrol here on the 10th of June. Two weeks ago yesterday. Would you have been working then? The Thursday.'

'Yeah. But I couldn't tell you who came in – a lot of visitors fill up here, there aren't that many places further up.'

'What about the CCTV?'

'God knows. My dad does all that.'

'Is he around?'

'No.'

'Do you know how long he keeps the tapes? How often they're changed?'

'No.'

'When will he be back?'

'Six, seven maybe.'

There was no point in me hanging around into the evening in the faint hope that a two-week-old videotape would not have been reused. Past experience told me most outlets re-used tape after a few days.

We were interrupted by a man in a smart suit, wearing one of those earpiece phones, who wanted to pay. I waited, feigning interest in the bags of sweets and air fresheners.

The young executive left the shop barking into his phone, 'We need it locked down by four and if she gets arsey then we're looking at Stevenage.'

Alone again, I showed the young woman the family photo of the Florins. Her eyes skated across it and she was on the brink of dismissing it when her stare fixed and her head tilted back a fraction. She peered closer then spoke slowly. 'Yes, she was here.'

Hope and excitement coursed through me.

'She wanted to buy two of the Jelly Bears, two the same.' She held her pen out, indicating the display of large, luridly coloured soft toys. They had saucer-like eyes and each one clutched a bag of sweets. 'But it's a new line and we'd only one of each design.' She looked again at the photo. 'Yeah, that's her.'

'Can you remember anything else? What she was wearing?'

She shook her head.

'The car?'

'No.'

'Was she in here on her own?'

'Yeah.' She cracked her gum again.

Janet must have been travelling with someone. Mark had their car and there was no evidence that she had hired a car. Besides, her driving licence was at home. Or was Mark with her? Had the Liverpool interview been a lie for the outside world allowing Janet and Mark a day in the Dales together. But only Mark comes back.

'Is there a railway station here?'

'No, the nearest is Settle.'

'When you saw her, was it morning or afternoon?'

She clicked her lip ring against her teeth, thought for a while. 'Morning. Because I told her I could order another Jelly Bear for the following day and we have to get orders in for noon. But she didn't want to do that. You said she's missing?'

'Yes.'

'And her kids?' She jerked her thumb towards the photo.

'At home with their dad.'

She pulled a face. 'Think she's run off with someone?'

'She might have. Look, will you ask your dad about the tapes – I'll leave my card and if he has anything from that day, please will you ask him to put it on one side and let me know?'

'OK.'

I took a note of their phone number and then asked her opinion about nearby hotels and restaurants. Which of those on my printout might appeal to a couple wanting a romantic meal? Which were open for lunch?

She talked me through the list – which places were drinking dens with pie and chips, which catered to the walkers, which looked pretty or were closed for refurbishment. Her local knowledge was a great way to prioritise. I thanked her for her help and tucked the paper away. At the exit, a thought struck me,

I turned and called back to her. 'Did she buy any Jelly Bears?'

'Yes. She got the lion and the tiger.'

Gifts for Isobel and Jacob. When was she planning to give them? Later that day when she went home? Or was she going to post them from some new life? Or save them for birthdays? I couldn't figure it out but one fact resounded clearly. The Thursday that Janet Florin had stopped for petrol here she'd been thinking about her children. A loving mum – just like everyone said she was.

Yorkshire people have a reputation for being close-mouthed and tight-fisted. Dour. Of the sample of hoteliers, bar staff and landlords I met about a third of them possessed the surly gene. With narrowing eyes and caustic glances they answered 'aye' or 'nay' to my enquires about Janet Florin. The pleasanter two-thirds elaborated but at the end of the afternoon and a tour of the main villages close to Grassington I'd not found any further sighting of her.

My mobile rang on the way back. I'd rigged up the hands-free set. It was Rachel. 'You were right,' she said. 'Berfan is in Wythenshawe Hospital, on the psych assessment unit. He was sectioned on Wednesday, but it took them long enough to get a name from him. Apparently, he'd been in town, creating a disturbance and got very agitated when the street wardens intervened. Thankfully, they realised he was mentally ill.'

Street wardens were a new addition to our forces for law and order. A visible presence in bright red jackets and official hats, they patrolled the city centre. People wanted more police on the beat but the modern force was stretched too thin to be used on foot patrols dealing with low-level incidents. The street wardens, with limited training and limited powers, bridged the gap.

'They took him in to the hospital.' Rachel finished.

'How is he?'

'Calmer now, they say. He's on medication. I've arranged for Ramin to visit tomorrow morning, ten-thirty, but I can't go with – I'm off on holiday, flight's later today. Could you give him a lift?'

'Of course.'

So Berfan had been losing it when he was seen begging in town and rambling about being a mythical blacksmith. Berfan had been roaming the streets for ten days, getting moved on, sleeping rough in all likelihood, begging for enough money to get a hot drink, his mind fragmenting. Ramin had insisted that Berfan was not sick. Now he would have to face the reality head on. I'd no idea how Berfan's illness would affect his asylum status. Would they wait for him to recover before sending him back to Iran? They'd have to, wouldn't they? He wouldn't be safe to travel if he was delusional or agitated.

Ramin was subdued, practically monosyllabic, on the phone when I rang him.

'It's a shame he's not well,' I said, 'but at least we know where he is now.'

'Yes.'

'And I'll see you in the morning, about quarter past ten.'

'Thank you.' He ended the call politely. He sounded numb, really, though it's hard to be sure when you're only getting 'yes' or 'no' down the line.

* * *

I'd told Ray not to cook me any tea so I made a cheese omelette and a side salad and polished that off. Then I helped Maddie with her homework. She had a worksheet to fill in comparing half a dozen different rocks or soils; what they felt like, looked like and were used for. We hunted round the house and garden until she'd found examples. Beat multiplication and division, any day.

Ray emerged from his workshop a while later, as Maddie was finishing the chart. 'Good trip?'

'Yes, worth going.'

There was a moment's awkwardness, we were both acutely aware of the recent intimacy we'd shared. If we'd been alone I'd probably have hugged or kissed him but neither of us was ready to express our new relationship in front of the children. He winked at me and that relieved the strain.

I talked to Diane after that. She'd spent the day googling breast cancer support sites. 'Information overload,' she complained.

'Useful?'

'Yes – just too much of it. And of course lots of different views. There's a group meets in Manchester, a drop-in, I'm thinking about going. You busy Monday?'

Please no, I thought. I want to help but I didn't want to be an interloper at that sort of gathering. 'To go to the group?' I said weakly.

'No,' she said scornfully. 'That's tomorrow. Monday night – come for tea.'

'Oh! Yes. Love to.'

*   *   *

I was emptying the dishwasher and yawning when Ray next found me.

'Tired?'

'Yeah, should be at self-defence, just haven't got the energy. I'm shattered.'

'Wonder why?' he teased.

I realised that there was a huge drawback to sleeping with your housemate – negotiating the pace of things. With a stranger, all the business of when to call, when to meet again is deliberated over – shall I ring, will he ring, etc. But without that distance, and therefore some control over contact, things were trickier. We saw each other every day. How were we to decide which days we'd be lovers? Thankfully, he saw my fatigue that evening was genuine and nothing to do with 'us'.

'You need an early night,' Ray said.

'That's the plan. And a long soak first.'

He smiled.

As I moved to go, he spoke again. 'Sal. It was OK, wasn't it?'

His question shocked me. Ray tends to avoid talking about emotional issues and it's rare he'll put himself in a vulnerable position. Throughout the preceding weeks when he'd first shown a romantic interest in me and then summarily dumped his girlfriend Laura, he'd never talked about what was going on beyond saying he wanted me – and that he knew the attraction wasn't all one sided. 'You feel it too,' he'd said.

Now, I looked at him: his deep brown eyes, his sculptured face, his arms olive-skinned and sinewy, the hairs straight and black.

'It was lovely,' I said. I waited a moment, gathering words. 'I don't know how we do this.'

'It'll work out.' He opened his arms then, spread them wide and I walked into his embrace and stood there for a few moments just enjoying the warmth.

CHAPTER FIFTEEN

Maddie woke me before the alarm. 'How do you get cancer?'

That brought me to full alert, pretty sharpish. I raised myself up, pushed my pillow against the headboard. I could tell from the band of light that edged my curtains that it was a sunny morning.

'Can I draw the curtains?' she asked. It happened quite often that telepathy or synchronicity between us. When she pulled them back, I could see high blue sky scored with chalky vapour trails.

'Scientists are still trying to find out more about cancer,' I told her. 'They know some things like smoking and drinking too much alcohol can cause it. Some cancers come when you get very old. There are things you can do to stay healthy.'

'Like five a day?'

School had been covering healthy eating recently.

'Yes, and plenty of exercise.'

She didn't ask any more so I left it at that. Maddie is the best judge of how much information she can handle.

After I'd taken the children to school, I spent an hour writing up notes on my trip. Halfway through, I got a call from a woman looking for someone to bug her secretary's office. Such activity was against the law, I explained. And evidence recovered like that couldn't be used in a prosecution. It wasn't a job I'd consider. When she persisted, I told her firmly that no, I couldn't recommend anyone else, either.

I relished the prospect of telling Trisha that I had found the start of a trail for Janet. But before I did, I would go and see Mark, confront him with the lies he'd told and see if there was a reasonable explanation. First, I had some hospital visiting to do.

Driving to pick up Ramin, I hit roadworks, which made me late. I sat in the car staring at billboards which promised heaven on earth if I only bought a mobile phone or a pair of designer jeans. There was a wall opposite the billboards that had been graffitied, a name tag and a crescent moon, a dragon. Graffiti was an offence but I preferred that offering to the legal stuff across the road. One thing I'd noticed, though, in my foray into the Yorkshire Dales was the beauty of a landscape not awash with signs and messages and visual clamour.

Ramin was subdued on the drive to Wythenshawe. Nervous, I assumed. I tried making conversation, explaining what I thought we would find at the hospital and he listened to what I said but didn't volunteer anything.

It took ages to find a parking space and then we had to pay £2 for the privilege. Wythenshawe is a huge hospital and it grew even more when they closed Withington, close to where I live.

The mental health wards were in an extension. The place

wasn't very different from Christie's where I'd been with Diane, though here security was more obvious with intercoms to enter the building. Ramin hung back a little as we reached the reception desk and I gave our names and Berfan's to the woman there.

'Just take a seat,' she invited us. 'I won't be a moment.' She walked off through the double doors that led to the wards.

It was very warm in the waiting area. The sun poured in through the glass doors and the synthetic smell of new carpet clung in the air. I helped myself to a glass of water from the machine and got one for Ramin. The water was very cold and tasted of aluminium, a thin metallic flavour.

'Would you like to follow me? Berfan's in the residents' lounge.' The receptionist took us along a couple of corridors, past a nurses' station and into a large square room which looked out onto a courtyard. The courtyard had yet to be landscaped but work had already been done to level the ground and piles of sharp sand and gravel sat hopefully in the corners.

In the lounge, chairs were set out around low coffee tables. A vending machine stood on one wall, a male nurse sat beside it. Berfan half rose when he saw his brother come into the room, then sat again, as though unsure of the convention. Berfan looked more like Ramin in real life than he had in the photograph. A smaller, skinnier version of his brother. His complexion was smooth, unlike Ramin's, though he had stubble along his jaw line and throat. His eyes were red and watery.

Ramin walked swiftly over to him and put his hands on his shoulders, stooping to greet him. Berfan stood again and the men hugged and patted each other on the back and Berfan began to cry. I was intruding. Slipping out of the room, I sat on one of the chairs in the corridor, leafing through a copy of *National Geographic* from the side table.

After about quarter of an hour, I looked in on them. Berfan was whispering agitatedly and Ramin sat forward at the edge of his chair as if trying to get a word in. The nurse seemed quite relaxed still; I assumed he'd intervene if Berfan needed help.

I spoke to him. 'Excuse me, are you with Berfan?'

'Yep. You family?'

'With his brother.' I didn't want to get bound up in confidentiality clauses. 'Do you know how he's doing? How long he'll be here?'

'Depends on his progress. They're still working on getting the medication right. That can take a while. Here's the doctor now.'

A young-looking woman with Mongolian features, dressed in a black trouser suit came into the room. Ramin and Berfan stood up.

'Good morning, I am Doctor Akstan – you are Berfan's family?'

'His brother.' Ramin patted his own chest. The doctor shook hands with him.

'I'm a friend,' I explained, 'helping Ramin to find Berfan.'

She nodded. 'Please, sit down.'

Berfan sat with us but he was whispering to himself, quietly and quickly. I got the impression of someone casting a spell. Something to ward off demons or crowd out unwelcome thoughts.

'I need to talk to you,' the doctor said to the brothers. She patted the file on her knee. 'We need to know Berfan's past history, to help us care for him now.'

'Here?' Ramin's eyes swerved round the room taking in me as well as the nurse.

The doctor was quick to grasp that he wanted more privacy and offered to take them to her office. The nurse followed them out. Ramin walked with his back taut and his fists clenched while Berfan shuffled his feet, head bowed and hands clasped tightly in front of him.

There's only so much *National Geographic* and *Cheshire Life* a woman can take. I did a bit of pacing, had a toilet break, decided what to buy for tea, got lost in a reverie about Ray and developed three design ideas for the courtyard area outside the windows (Mexican, Rainforest Grotto and Chinese Water Garden).

When the three of them came back, I asked the doctor the same question that I'd asked the nurse, and got a similar reply; depends on how he does with the medication. 'Come as often as you can,' she told Ramin.

Berfan was beginning to rock to and fro, his hands wrapped tight about his body. I sensed the coming separation was making him anxious and I didn't want to drag it out.

'Goodbye, Berfan,' I said. 'We'll see you soon.'

I stepped aside as Ramin embraced him. I heard a gusty sob from Berfan and felt my own throat close in sympathy. Thanking Doctor Akstan, we shook hands and she waited to accompany Berfan back to the ward.

Ramin thrust his hands into the front pockets of his jeans and strode purposefully alongside me to the exit. His face was pinched, his cheeks drawn in.

We drove up Princess Parkway, towards the city, past Southern Cemetery and then the Siemens building; its cool sugar cube lines easy on the eye.

As we waited at the lights at Moss Side, I offered to take Ramin to visit again.

'No. It's fine. You found him, thank you. There is a bus.'

'I'm happy to drive.'

'No.'

I didn't press it. 'Did the doctor say what's wrong? Is it depression?'

'I know what's wrong,' he said bitterly.

'But I thought you said...'

'Please.' He flattened his hand a few inches from his own head, a barrier. Enough, shut up, leave me alone.

It was awkward, this relationship. Ramin patently didn't want to confide in me and his response to my questions made me feel clumsy and insensitive.

In Longsight, I parked outside the house. A trio of lads on bikes, hoodies up circled the end of the street and sized us up before moving off.

Ramin thanked me and opened the door.

'If I can help again, please call me. I hope he's better soon.'

He nodded. Repeated his thanks and extended his hand. I shook it. Our hands were practically the same size.

It felt like an unsatisfactory parting. Left me curious and ill at ease. What had he meant when he said he knew what was wrong? Had Berfan been ill like this before? He's not crazy, he had insisted when the prospect had been raised. I assumed I'd not see Ramin or his brother again. My job done. I got that one wrong. Bigtime.

CHAPTER SIXTEEN

The prospect of tackling Mark Florin shadowed me over that weekend. Perhaps I should go straight to the police with my doubts. After all, he had lied to them as well as everyone else. But I was reluctant to start pointing fingers at someone who hadn't had chance to account for themselves. It would be horrible if I landed him in it and then found there was some innocent reason behind the falsehood.

Monday morning and Bob Swithinbank perched his considerable weight on the sofa in my office and leant forward, his face intent and one foot tapping. 'So she's in Wythenshawe,' he said.

'Yes, Northern Moor. Do you know it?'

'I grew up in Sale – just next door. Bit different, though.'

I nodded. Sale was a wealthier area. 'I don't know whether her husband's still around. Like I said, there are two children – teenagers.'

His face was alive with excitement.

'The girl's sixteen, she's called Susan. I haven't any details for the boy yet, he looks a bit older.'

'You said Sandra thought the letter was from the council?'

'She's in arrears, apparently. There was a stack of unopened mail. I think she has some trouble reading. She asked me to tell her what the letter said.'

He gave a little murmur of sympathy.

I described in as much detail as possible the few minutes I'd spent with Sandra. Bob grinned at the mention of the cats but when he heard about her denial he dipped his head, shaking it so that the rings that edged his ears jiggled.

'She doesn't want to know.' He gave a noisy sigh and sat back, his T-shirt stretching across his beer belly. He rubbed at his face.

'She was completely overwhelmed,' I explained. 'It's a common first reaction: panic, fear, denial. You've been a secret all her life, her kids don't know, her husband, friends. What will they think of her? And it stirs up painful memories. An awful time in her life.'

'Having me.' For a moment, he was a child, bristling with bitter resentment.

'Losing you.' I paused. 'She did say something as I was leaving: *he mustn't come here.*'

Bob flinched.

'No, it's an admission, you see,' I carried on. 'She was anxious about it and she couldn't keep up the pretence of you not existing. I think if you give her time, she'll be curious. And she'll realise that you want to see her. She probably imagines you're angry with her for the adoption. That you hate her for it. A lot of women feel terribly guilty about what they've done; they hope it's been for the best, that's what everyone told them, but they never know. Now she's learnt that you want to contact her, it's a sort of reassurance. I asked her to think about it and ring me whenever she was ready.'

'If I could just call her,' he swayed forward, frustration etched in his voice.

'You risk frightening her off. Ask anyone involved in adoption and reunion and they'll tell you door-stepping someone, getting in touch directly out of the blue, is the worst possible way to go about it. It's best to use an intermediary. There was a danger my visit would backfire, I hope it hasn't. But it would have been a disaster for her if that had been you. She couldn't have handled it.'

He was looking sceptical.

'Think about it, how long did it take you from first thinking about tracing your birth mother to coming here?'

He gave a wry smile. 'Years.'

'Why?'

'OK. Point taken. But it's hard now I know she's really there, and so close.'

'And for her.'

'What's she look like?'

I described Sandra as best as I could. He drank it all in.

'I was only a couple of miles away,' he said. 'I wasn't allowed to set foot in Wythenshawe, though.' He hesitated. 'Do you think that'll be a problem – me some posh bloke with a music degree?'

Surveying his sprawling bulk, the metal face furniture and long hair and hearing the grate of his Mancunian accent, I laughed aloud. 'Posh doesn't quite do it.' I shrugged. 'Who can say? You might meet once, have nothing in common and leave it at that. You might grow close. Or something in between.'

'Or nothing.'

I couldn't gainsay him. I spread my hands wide. It was in the hands of the fates.

He looked my way. 'Now, it's a waiting game.'

'Yes.'

Bob wanted to settle his account. Once he'd written me a cheque, he spoke again: 'She didn't ask anything about me?' His eyes were bright and he cracked at his knuckles.

'She was stunned,' I reminded him.

He was silent for a moment, keeping his disappointment in check. 'Do you think she'll ring?' He spoke quietly.

'Hard to say but I hope so.'

I hadn't been home long when Diane called to rearrange dinner. An old friend of hers was visiting Manchester and she wanted to make time to see her. We put it in for the following week. I'd no sooner replaced the receiver than it rang again. Had Diane forgotten something? I snatched it up. 'Hello?'

It was Trisha Marlowe. 'They've arrested Mark,' she said, fighting tears. 'They've found Janet. She's been killed. They found her in the bottom of a quarry, in a place called Coverdale.'

It hit me like a blow to the stomach, strong enough to force me out of my chair. I felt sick. My mind flew back over the case: the toys she'd bought her children, the snapshots at the house, her friend Trisha worried for her, the life of leisure she'd joked about. Janet Florin was now lying broken on the rocks, her dark rose trouser suit muddy and bloodstained, her new shoes scuffed.

'Trisha, I'm so sorry. Where are you?'

'Home.'

'I'll come over, OK?'

'Thanks.'

My bowels churned and I felt the skittering of panic inside. Sweat coated the back of my neck and trickled down my sides. Consciously, I steadied myself, holding onto the table edge for support for a few moments. I went and got a glass of water and sipped it. From the kitchen cupboard, I got the little bottle of Rescue Remedy that I sometimes use to settle the kids. With the pipette, I squeezed four drops onto my tongue. The festive brandy taste made my mouth water. After using the loo, I filled the washbasin and splashed cold water on my face but my stomach was still a ball of tension.

I got the road atlas, struggled to open it, my hands were trembling so badly. Coverdale was a few miles north-west of Grassington. Janet wasn't missing anymore – she was dead. My thoughts flew to Mark, who'd reported her disappearance but had given a false account of his movements that day. Had he driven Janet to Grassington then killed her and dumped her in the quarry? Why? Had he discovered her affair? Learnt that Monday night yoga classes were a façade to conceal her adultery? Or had he killed her for financial gain, knowing her life assurance would relieve their crippling debts? Had he thought that the body wouldn't be found?

Being close to death inevitably calls up primitive instincts: the visceral surge of adrenalin, fuelled by the impulse for self-preservation. It also rouses more complex responses: the emotions of shame and guilt. The what-ifs and should-I-haves. In all likelihood, Janet had been killed before I even met her friend or family but I still played the game of reassuring myself that I hadn't been culpable or negligent.

Picking up my car keys and bag, and setting the answerphone, I headed out of the house. I didn't get very far. There were two detectives on the doorstep. They wanted to question me about the murder of Janet Florin.

Due to my work, I've more experience than most people of dealing with the police. It's varied wildly. I've dealt with the lazy, the incompetent and the bigoted as well as the committed, brave and compassionate. But one thing is a constant: they have the authority. They have the power to arrest people and charge them. Their pursuit can lead to someone's incarceration. The excesses of corruption that characterised the Seventies seem to have been eradicated but how scary is the prospect that you might get the rotten apple, the one with their own warped agenda. Talking to the police about a serious crime is daunting. And the very situation can make you feel that you're slightly out of line, not totally innocent. Maybe it comes from their body language or the way questions are phrased, or perhaps it's down to the fact that we have nearly all broken the law one way or another (no, I'm not saying) but it's an unnerving undercurrent.

In this case, the undercurrent was smothered by civility. Detective Constable Whittaker did most of the talking. She smiled a lot, fleeting flashes of teeth like a sympathetic nurse. She was built like an ox and had huge hands which dwarfed the pen she used to make notes. Her navy linen suit was wrinkled and misshapen and gave an impression of exhaustion rather than crisp office wear. Her colleague was a slim, neat Chinese guy, DC Tan who looked dapper in a dazzling white shirt and charcoal-coloured tie.

They declined drinks, they let me call Trisha and let her

know I wouldn't be coming and then they got down to business, seated at my kitchen table.

Whittaker began by asking me about how I'd been hired. She noted my answers then asked, 'And Mr Florin, he knew about Mrs Marlowe's plan?'

'Yes, he was—' I hesitated, anxious to be accurate and not let the morning's revelations colour my memories. 'He was reasonably helpful at first. He talked to me, gave me copies of their bank statements and credit card bills.'

'How would you describe his state of mind?'

'He was a bit...prickly. Irritable.' I recalled Steve Marlowe saying Mark Florin had a permanent chip on his shoulder. 'I found out he lied to me.'

Whittaker glanced up sharply. Tan pressed his palms together. He had beautifully manicured nails. An image of Ray stroking my shoulder, trailing his fingers down my spine disturbed me. I took a sip of water and cleared my throat. Whittaker waited for me to continue.

'The day Janet went missing, Mark had a job interview at a firm in Liverpool. When I rang to confirm it, they told me there hadn't been any interviews. I don't know where he was but Janet was seen in Grassington that day, late in the morning.'

It took another hour and a half for Whittaker to record all the information I had. She was meticulous about detail and went through everything with a fine-tooth comb: fleshing things out, getting me to elaborate on statements or observations. She asked me several times whether I had any idea who Janet Florin might have been involved with. I began to wonder whether she thought I was hiding the knowledge from her.

My shoulder and neck were burning with tension by the end of the interview.

'We need to write this up as a full statement,' Whittaker explained. 'Then you need to read it, correct any errors and sign it.'

She wrote it, a sentence at a time, and checked with me. Being a formal document, it was littered with stock police phrases that would never roll lightly off the tongue of any ordinary citizen. Things like *upon retuning to my home I had reason to question Mr Florin's account*, or, *having ascertained that my client had no prior knowledge of an extra-marital liaison*.

'You have notes of your own,' Whittaker asked once the statement was completed.

'Yes.'

'We'd appreciate it if we can take those for examination.'

'Of course, I'll make copies.'

'We'll need the originals.'

'Right, erm… Now?'

She flashed another bright smile.

'There's a copier at the newsagents,' I said.

They accompanied me to the shop. I felt ridiculous. OK, it was just procedure but the escort implied I might not be trustworthy and could subvert their request for my notes.

Mohammed, the shopkeeper, greeted me warmly and began to chat about objections to a local planning application for luxury apartments on a tiny vacant lot. My lukewarm reply and sideways glance at the police sent him back to watching the test match on television.

'What about Isobel and Jacob?' I asked the detectives once we were back at the house.

'Social Services will be arranging for care. Hopefully with friends or family.'

'Trisha Marlowe is their godmother.'

Whittaker nodded. Was Trisha being questioned now, as well? Would she be capable of looking after the children? Janet's father was dead and her mother was estranged, she had emigrated. There hadn't been brothers or sisters. I didn't know about Mark's family. What was the etiquette in a situation like this? If Mark was charged with murdering his wife, would it affect whether his relatives could have custody of the children?

CHAPTER SEVENTEEN

Once the police had gone, I didn't know what to do with myself. Trisha's phone was engaged when I tried and her mobile was switched off. Was I hungry – was the hollow feeling just from shock? It would be wise to eat a little something so I buttered a slice of bread, smeared it with honey and had a cup of Darjeeling with it. I was too jittery for coffee.

Switching on the radio, I caught the news report: *'The body of a woman recovered earlier today from an abandoned quarry in the Dales National Park is said by North Yorkshire police to be that of thirty-four-year-old Janet Florin, who has been missing from the family home for two weeks. Police have launched a murder inquiry. Mrs Florin, a teacher from Manchester, is married with two small children. A man is helping police with their inquiries.'*

The television had much the same script but it was accompanied by a photo of Janet and some footage from the quarry with police tape fluttering in the breeze and people in protective blue suits at work.

Thinking of Jacob and Isobel, my eyes pricked. I blew my nose, cleared my throat.

It was high summer and the dazzling light and burning heat seemed to mock the dark tragedy. I couldn't sit still inside and

I couldn't face people so I retreated to the garden with a trowel and began weeding. Dandelion and dock, chickweed and buttercup had spread throughout the flower borders. The sun was fierce and I put on cream so I wouldn't burn. Strawberries were fruiting, most were still green and white but some were tinged with pink. The garden was laden with bees bobbing here and there among the blooms and the air was thick with dozens of fluffy seeds which drifted lazily like unseasonal snow. Voices rang out from down the street: some workmen shouting to each other, snatches of television and bursts of rap music punctuating the constant symphony of traffic: the screech and rumble of buses, the rattle of taxis, whining motorbikes and the drone of cars.

My mind wheeled back time and again to the Florins. If Mark was found guilty of Janet's murder, how could their children ever overcome that legacy? To lose a parent is awful; to lose one to violence worse but to lose one parent through the violence of the other is just devastating.

How had she died? They hadn't released the details yet. Perhaps they were still trying to establish the cause of death.

At two o'clock, I tipped the heap of weeds into the compost bin and went in to wash my hands. Taking a drink of cranberry and ice outside, I dragged a sun-lounger out from the shade, reapplied cream and lay there. The act itself seemed bizarre in the circumstances but it was testament to my sense of dislocation. The heavy heat after the physical work helped me to relax a little. I could smell the medicinal aroma from the eucalyptus tree and that along with the chink of ice in my drink and the coconut smell of sun lotion reminded me of foreign holidays. Transport me there, I thought, some

Mediterranean island for a month or so.

A cat stalked along the wall at the bottom of the garden, its tail held high for balance. A fire engine howled, its sound growing louder then receding as it raced along the main road. I drained my tumbler and sucked the ice cubes until my teeth hurt then spat them back in the glass.

Movement caught my eye, the surface of the pond jostled and then two bulbous eyes, the curve of a head appeared.

'Hello, frog,' I said aloud. Pleasure bloomed in my chest. It was a good feeling. Eclipsing everything else for a moment.

Collecting the children, it was soon apparent that the heat made them fractious. Maddie walked more and more slowly until she was dragging each foot, scraping the toes of her shoes along the way. A move calculated to wind me up as well as destroy her footwear. But today I wasn't going to get riled. It seemed preposterous more than anything.

'There are lollies in the freezer,' I bribed her, 'and we can fill the paddling pool. But if you spoil your shoes doing that,' keeping my voice level, 'then I'll have to use your pocket money to buy new ones.' She did it twice more so as not to lose face and then walked normally.

The kids had beans on toast for tea, I made ratatouille for Ray and me, and neither of the children would touch aubergines or courgettes. They ate fast and ran back out to the paddling pool as soon as they'd finished.

'Hey,' Ray stretched his hand across the table to me. His greeting half a question. He'd picked up on my mood.

'Work,' I grimaced. 'The woman I've been searching for has been found. She's been murdered.'

'Oh, Jesus.' He retracted his hand, sat up straight.

'The police have been here. They've arrested the husband. She was probably dead all along.' I'd been looking for a dead woman.

'How come he hired you?'

'Her friend did.'

'And he didn't object?'

'No. He didn't like it all that much but he went along with it.'

'Maybe he didn't want to protest too much,' Ray suggested. 'I'm sorry. Heavy stuff.'

I nodded. He got up and walked round to me, stood behind me and placed his hands on my shoulders, bent and kissed the top of my head.

Maddie yelled outside and Tom sang a snatch of a song. Digger barked once.

'I could do you a massage later,' he murmured in my ear.

'Or something stronger,' I said hoarsely.

'That can be arranged.'

I swivelled round to face him, raising my lips to his. The kiss was fleeting, teasing enough to make me giddy with desire.

We sat out on the patio later, waiting until the children were asleep, watching the evening fade to rose, then dove grey, then deepen. We shared a very cold bottle of sauvignon blanc. Like teenagers we touched and teased and kissed and stroked until we were mad for more. My head was light and buzzy, my body aching for satisfaction, everything taut and tingling and hungry.

Wordlessly, we went indoors, stopping in the hall, on the

stairs, on the landing for another kiss. Pressing our bodies close, communicating too with jerky little breaths and soft murmurs.

Our lovemaking was greedy and urgent. I came soaring on a wave, cresting high then tumbling down to sweet relief. Becalmed with the thudding of my heart and his lazy, breathless smile.

Trisha Marlowe rang me again early the following morning.

'I can't believe it,' she said. 'I just can't believe it. I know it's a cliché but it really is like a dream, like a nightmare and I can't wake up.'

'I'm so sorry,' I told her. 'It's a terrible thing to happen.'

'The police are still talking to Mark. Do you think he...could he do that? Why? Why would he do that?'

'I don't know.' I said. Though I had some theories. But at that point it was more important to give Trisha a chance to talk, than for me to play detective. 'It may just be routine. They always have to speak with close family, you know. Often they just need to eliminate them.' And often they charge them.

'Jacob and Isobel are here. They don't know what's hit them.' Trisha's voice broke and I could hear her choking back tears.

'Would you like me to come over?'

'Please. I don't know who else I can talk to.'

The weather held and the car was stifling, my back and thighs were sticky against the seat. With the windows open and the fan on I created a hot breeze, like some desert wind. The road ahead shimmered and rippled in the heat.

The crunching of gravel as I drove into their curving drive announced my arrival at the Marlowes' and brought Jacob and Isobel running from a tepee made of canes and sheeting. The children regarded me solemnly as I got out of the car. Trisha opened the door and she and Steve came outside. She looked drawn but made the effort to sound cheerful when she told the children I had come for a meeting and would they like more juice or another biscuit.

'Yes,' Isobel nodded, 'and crisps.' Jacob remained stony faced. My heart went out to him, that fearful bravery. He was eight. When had he learnt to retreat like that, to choke back his emotions?

'I'll get it,' Steve offered, nodding at me by way of greeting. He looked tired too and sounded husky. I imagined the couple had been awake half the night trying to make sense of what was happening.

With its expansive glass frontage, I'd expected the house to be like an oven but awnings shielded the living area from the glare of the sun and the water streaming down one of the glass screens added a fresh, cool feel to the place.

The room bore witness to the children's arrival, with toys, items of clothing and crayons scattered about. A completed Lego kit of Star Wars – top of the range and the sort of thing Tom longed for but never got – graced the coffee table.

'Would you like a drink?' Steve asked from the kitchen doorway. 'We've fresh lemonade.'

'That sounds lovely, thanks.'

'Darling?'

'No, I'm fine,' said Trisha.

She motioned for me to sit.

'How are they?' I asked.

'Bewildered,' she said. 'I've told them about Janet. That she won't be coming home, that she's dead.' Her voice fell to a whisper as she said the word. 'They've both cried a bit. Isobel keeps asking questions. *Why? What happened?*' Trisha shook her head. 'Do you think he did it?'

'I don't know.'

Steve came in and passed me a drink, ice cubes clinking. Trisha held her hand out to him and he took it and sat down beside her.

'I said to Steve,' Trisha began, 'I just can't believe it – it won't sink in. To think that he—' Her voice rose dangerously and she pressed her hands to her face. Steve tried to calm her, shushing her and stroking the back of her neck.

I sipped at the cloudy lemonade. It was tangy, sharp and fizzy, and cleared the dryness from my throat.

'The police spoke to me yesterday,' I said. 'I told them what I'd found out about Janet: the probability that she was involved with someone else.'

Trisha gave a nod. 'But she wasn't running away, was she? She didn't take anything with her.'

'No, she didn't. And Mark wasn't in Liverpool that day.'

'What?' Trisha's eyes darkened and a frown furrowed between them.

'The job interview?' Steve queried.

'It didn't happen – I checked.'

Trisha absorbed this for a moment and then rounded on me. 'Why didn't you tell me?'

'I thought it was important to give Mark a chance to clarify things first – to see if there was a simple explanation.'

'Oh, yes,' she retorted, her dark eyes flaring. 'Like he was killing his wife, you mean?' A gust of grief interrupted her rage at me.

'I didn't get the chance to ask him,' I said.

'This man she was seeing,' Trisha said, biting down on her anger, 'maybe he doesn't exist. We've no proof, have we? She never mentioned him to me. Maybe all that's just a wild goose chase.'

'It is conjecture,' I admitted. 'The Monday nights, dropping her hair appointment. She could just have chosen to switch salon. Been joking when she hinted at a new beginning. We all talk about winning the lottery. But where was she when she was supposed to be at yoga? Seeing someone was the most obvious answer.'

'Maybe not the right one,' she said. 'The police suspect Mark, after all.' She gave a shudder. 'I can't stop thinking about what it must have been like. If she was frightened or tried to get away. Whether she struggled. They haven't even said what happened to her, how she died. Was she raped? I keep thinking of her—' her words became jerky, her breath irregular, 'of Janet really scared and being stabbed or strangled or something and knowing that she's going to die. Do you think she knew?'

'Trish, don't,' Steve said gently.

'I don't want to think like that,' she told him, 'I just can't help it. I loved her and this is so awful.'

'It might be easier when we know what happened.' I tried to reassure her. It sounds barmy but there's a finality comes from having the facts. For now Trisha was at the mercy of her imagination and envisaging the very worst.

The clatter of the children coming in from the garden echoed off the wooden floors and walls. Trisha tried to rearrange her expression. Jacob picked up a PSP from a chair and began thumbing at it, peering down and ignoring us all. Isobel climbed into Trisha's lap and touched Trisha's face, giving it a little pat, before nestling down. The little girl began to suck her thumb, her index finger stroking her nose. She looked flushed, her eyes heavy. All the signs of a child needing sleep.

Our conversation ground to a halt. 'Please let me know if you hear anything,' I said.

Steve and Trisha both nodded. Steve rose. 'I'll see you out.'

In the sunshine, he stood with his hands in his pockets, looking out at the broad sweep of hills, their flanks green and brown, suede smooth in the clear light. I opened the car.

'Thank you,' he said. 'She's very upset,' he added apologetically.

'It's terrible,' I replied. 'Trisha and Janet – they were very close. It's an awful thing.' I thought of Diane and me – darted from the thought.

CHAPTER EIGHTEEN

At lunchtime, the detective leading the enquiry made an appeal to the public for information. I watched it on television. He revealed that Janet Florin had drowned and had sustained serious head injuries that had contributed to her death. Drowned? Had she been killed elsewhere and then been thrown onto the rocks in the quarry? Apparently not. The detective elaborated. The bottom of the quarry was flooded and the water deep. Her head injuries appeared to have been sustained before she entered the water. Anyone who had seen Janet on Thursday 10th of June was urged to contact the police. In answer to a question from a journalist, the policeman said that Mr Florin was helping with their enquiries but he refused to be drawn any further.

Murder is savage. Drowning, head injuries. I dwelt on the details as I walked round to my office. It smelt fusty in the heat. I unlocked and opened the narrow window and set to work closing my file on Janet Florin. I calculated my hours and prepared an invoice for Trisha. It felt heartless. I'd an impulse to write it off but I couldn't afford a sentimental gesture – this was my livelihood. Not as if the Marlowes were strapped for cash. However, I would retain the bill until it was an appropriate time to send it. When things weren't so raw.

After I'd dealt with my correspondence, I walked up to the bank in Withington to pay in my cheque from Bob. The boards outside the paper shop declared *Murdered Mum Drowned*. I thought work would help to ground me but I couldn't shake off the sensation of dread. I needed to talk to someone. Ray was at work and I hadn't talked to him much about the case anyway – we'd been otherwise occupied. As it is, there's always been some tension between us about my job. He dislikes the risks it brings and I chafe at his concern. Would the new phase in our relationship make that even worse?

Diane was home and invited me round when I called her.

'You're not working?' I checked.

'Nope, baking.'

'Yum, yum.'

'Crikey!' When I got there, the tiny kitchen was chock-a-block with cakes, pies, pasties. The air smelt of biscuits. 'You going wholesale?'

'Stocking up. Freeze most of it and use them up when I don't feel like cooking.'

'You always feel—' I stopped. Groaned, feeling crass. It was the practical details of Diane's illness and the imminent treatment that brought it slamming home each time. Aspects I hadn't given a thought to – Diane lived alone, she'd be weak and sick at times if she ended up having chemotherapy following surgery, and not capable of making a meal.

'Coffee?'

'Thanks. Stay with us,' I invited her. 'Honestly. No one's in the attic flat.'

'Christ, no. I want peace and quiet, not screaming kids.'

Diane wasn't fond of children. Nothing personal, just she'd never felt the need to have any (her own or other people's) in her life.

'I'll come here then,' I offered.

She began to object but I interrupted. 'I will – just to keep things ticking over. Maybe not twenty-four hours a day but we'll see what you need.'

She grunted. The nearest I'd get to an agreement.

'Have a piece.' She nodded at the food.

'Ta.' I helped myself to a slab of parkin, dark and sticky. An odd choice for a summer's day; we usually have it around bonfire night when the leaves are falling and there's a nip in the air.

She slid a tray of pasties into the oven and closed the door. Made coffee in the cafetière which we took outside.

Diane's two-up, two-down only has a small backyard but she's transformed it, using it as a palette to experiment with different artistic techniques and materials. The walls are covered with broken tile, mirror and wood reminiscent of Gaudi's style. Here and there, she's incorporated planters so there are splashes of greenery. The floor is done with mosaics like a Roman villa. Above is a bamboo pergola. I'd given her a tree for her birthday one year – a honey locust tree with delicate, lacy vivid green leaves. The branches cascade down over the pergola giving dappled shade in the summer.

'How was the group?' I asked her.

'Weird. Bit depressing actually. Not going back there again.'

'You could take some cakes – cheer them up.'

'But,' she paused, tilted her head, 'I have decided to go for the lumpectomy. I mean,' she weighed her breasts in her palms, 'imagine the scale of reconstruction.'

I laughed. 'Good.' I bit into the parkin, savoured the moist, springy texture, tasted ginger and rich treacle. Took a swallow of coffee. Diane studied me, saying nothing. She messed with her hair, hunching up the extensions and letting them fall. She kept staring.

'What?' I asked her.

'That's my line,' she said. 'You don't usually call round in the daytime.'

I held my hands up in surrender. 'You heard about the woman who's been murdered?'

She shook her head. 'New regime: no news – too negative.'

'Ah. Never mind then.'

'You can't leave me hanging.'

'It's grim,' I warned her.

'Go on.'

'I was looking for her – she was missing. Now they've found her.'

'Aw, God.'

'Bashed over the head and drowned in a quarry. They're questioning her husband.'

'That's awful.'

We sat in silence for a moment, each contemplating such a brutal death.

'I thought I wanted to talk about it but now I'm here—'

'Not because of me?'

'No, no. Just…' I thought there was nothing else to say but then found myself opening up to Diane. Describing the Marlowes to her, and the Florins, their children, the tiny clues

I'd had when I was searching for her, the shock when I'd first heard the news, the visit from the police. Then I told her about Berfan, looking for him in town and finding him on the psychiatric ward. By the time I was done, we needed a refill of coffee and seconds of parkin.

'On the positive side...' I started.

'What?'

My cheeks grew hot.

'Ray!' she breathed.

I did a reasonable Cheshire cat impression.

'When?'

'Thursday and...last night.'

'Back for more, eh? Mind you, you've practically been a nun these last few years. And the moustache?'

I laughed, nearly choking on a mouthful of coffee. 'I'm getting used to it.' I looked up at the filigree leaves. 'I'm trying not to think about the future: whether it's serious, what it all means...'

'...whether you'll wear white.'

I shoved her. 'Taking your advice, go with the flow.'

'Is it working?'

'For now. Mind you, all this other stuff, work being so horrible—'

'Too busy worrying about that instead?' she asked.

'Yeah.' God, I love this woman, I thought. I could share anything with her, be honest, be vulnerable and she understands and supports me. 'We ought to do something together,' I said, the idea blooming in my mind. 'Something special after the surgery.'

'In between the chemo. When I'm not clutching a sick bowl.'

'Yep. A trip somewhere.'

'Blackpool?'

'Be serious. We haven't been away anywhere together since I had Maddie.'

'*Away* away,' she said. 'You in the money?'

'I can pay my half, look for a bargain.' In the past, Diane's income had fluctuated as much as mine had. More so sometimes. But the last couple of years had seen a steady stream of commissions and residencies come her way as well as her own show. She was in demand. With her mortgage paid off and no dependents, she was relishing the novelty of being solvent.

'Yeah, all right,' she agreed. 'No camping though.'

'Promise.'

Thursday morning, as I was loading the washing machine, my mobile went. I didn't recognise the caller's number. 'Hello, it's Sandra, Sandra Patefield.' Bob Swithinbank's birth mother. 'You said I could ring you.' She sounded defensive. I imagined it had taken her a lot of nerve to make the call. 'There's something I want to talk to you about.'

'Would you like me to come round?'

'Yeah, thanks. When?' Anxiety in the last question.

'Half an hour?'

'Yeah, that's fine, thanks.'

It was a good sign and I felt a fillip at the prospect of a positive outcome to one of my cases.

Their garden looked the same, even down to the cat sprawled across the same piece of scrap-iron baking in the sun. Sandra let me in. 'Do you want a brew?'

'Tea, thanks, just milk.' I accepted in part to give her a little space to gather her thoughts.

'I've not slept since you came,' she said bluntly. 'Sit down, I'll bring it through.'

She was quick, must have had it all lined up ready. I took the mug and put it on the side table. She scooped a kitten off her chair and slowly lowered herself into it. She'd coloured her hair since my last visit, black roots replaced by buttery yellow. She wore a long, loose turquoise kaftan with three-quarter length sleeves embroidered around the neckline and cuffs with silver thread.

'Like being struck by lightning,' she said. 'My heart went like the clappers.'

'It's a big shock,' I acknowledged.

'So, he got you to look for me?'

'That's right.'

'And he's called Bob?'

'Bob Swithinbank, Robert. You called him Matthew.'

Her face softened. 'Yes. I never thought...my kids don't know. Gary,' she tipped her chin towards the picture on the wall, 'he's in Iraq. Joined up as soon as he left school.'

'How long has he been out there?'

'This is his second tour. Did six months last year. I didn't want him to go back, didn't want him to go in the first place. It's a right bloody mess, isn't it? He's another two months then he's home.'

'You must worry about him.'

'Yes. He says it's not so bad where he is but then it's getting worse everywhere far as I can see.' She sighed. 'Susan's two years younger. She's bright, staying on in sixth form.'

'And your husband?'

'Hah! Long gone.' She snorted. 'One less kid to worry about.' Her tone changed as she asked me 'What's he like? What's he look like?'

'I have a photograph, a recent one, if you'd like to see it.'

She nodded, her face stark with trepidation. I passed her the snapshot. It had been taken at a festival in Sweden. An outside shot, blurred figures behind him, Bob was grinning at the camera, his expression genuine rather than posed. He wore a white T-shirt with a Chinese dragon stencilled onto it, jeans, a broad-rimmed leather hat.

'Oh!' Sandra gave a little cry when she saw him. 'He's like our Colin – my brother. Same sort of face. If you put them in the same clothes. He likes his piercings, doesn't he? Is he tall?'

'Six foot.'

She blinked. 'I think of him as a baby. Daft, isn't it? All grown up. Thirty he was in February and I think of him as a newborn.' She went very still. She closed her eyes and tightened her mouth. After a minute, she stretched out her arm to give me the picture back.

'You can keep it,' I told her.

'Thanks,' she whispered.

'Perhaps you've one of yourself I could pass on to Bob?'

'Well, I don't know.' She thought for a moment. 'We've got some holiday snaps. Hang on.' She removed the kitten and crossed to the sideboard, opened a drawer and pulled out a luridly coloured envelope of photos. 'I keep meaning to sort them out, put them in an album, but I never do.'

There was knocking at the door and a voice called out 'Sandra, are you coming down the precinct?'

She froze. She turned to me and mimed I should keep quiet. My car was outside so her visitor would know she had company. Sandra went out of the sitting room closing the door behind her. 'I'm tied up; I've someone here about a loan.'

'Not from Gerrity's are they?'

'No.'

''Cos you need to steer clear of them, rob you blind, they will. Our Vicky's still up to her eyeballs with them.'

'They're not from Gerrity's,' Sandra said sharply.

'All right, keep yer 'air on. Catch you later, then.'

The door closed.

Sandra returned. She stood and rifled through the batch of photos. 'There's that one – wedding last year.'

She passed it and I nodded with approval. She was wearing a floral two-piece and a straw hat and stood near a large floral arrangement. She looked blowsy and happy. 'That's great.'

She returned the photos to the drawer, half closed it then changed her mind. Drew out a large parchment album. She sat down with this and turned the pages. 'There,' she passed the heavy book to me. 'That was just before I found out I was expecting.'

A bonny schoolgirl in a mini-dress.

'And the next page.'

I turned over.

'That was the Christmas after I had him.' She was sitting on a sofa, Christmas wrapping paper all over the floor. She wore jeans and a glittery top, a half-smile on her lips. How tough must it have been for her to go along with the festive celebrations just weeks after leaving her baby.

'How old were you there?'

'Seventeen. You can give him that an' all, if you like.'

'Yes. Thank you.'

I handed back the album so she could take the photo out of the cellophane cover. An image sprang to mind, of Jacob and Isobel Florin looking at pictures of Janet, her life frozen in time. Janet and Mark as students, carrying backpacks, Janet squinting into the sun, a broad smile on her face, the four of them together at Jacob's eighth birthday party, the last one she'd share. The mother they could barely remember.

'What does he do?' Sandra asked. 'Is he working?'

'He plays music for a living.'

'Does he? He in an orchestra or something?'

'A rock band.'

'Bloody hell. What they called.'

'Crashbucket.'

She shook her head. 'Is he married?'

'No. He's got a girlfriend, though.'

She put one fist to her mouth as she shook her head. 'I can't take it in.' The kitten began clawing at her dress by her ankles, its tiny claws snagging on the cotton. 'Oy.' She pulled it up and set it on her lap.

'He likes cats,' I told her.

'I can't see him,' she said in a rush. 'You'll have to explain. There's no way I can tell the kids. I'm glad he's all right. You do wonder. You always wonder.'

'You don't need to decide now,' I said. 'Bob knows you need time. It's best for everyone to take it nice and slowly. It might be months before you feel ready to talk to him on the phone. But Bob wanted you to have his mobile number, in case you ever do want to speak to him.' I gave her a small card with it written on.

'I think it's best left in the past,' she said emphatically. 'Just tell him I'm glad he's all right.'

'OK. And thanks for these. He'll be delighted.'

As soon as I got back to my office, I rang Bob and told him about meeting Sandra. He was by turns elated at the new titbits of information and despondent at her not wanting to meet him, or call him yet. He rallied when I told him about the photos and he begged me to post them on to him first class. 'She won't ring, will she?'

'She might.' It was the best I could do. And all he could do was live in hope.

CHAPTER NINETEEN

Mr Stefanos said he was delighted that Diane had made her decision, though it was hard to believe him because he still looked so glum. He discussed with us what the surgery would involve and told Diane that in all likelihood they would schedule her an appointment within two weeks.

He talked about the factors that would influence any follow-up treatment. Again there seemed to be a wide range of options and it wasn't a given that she'd need any medication at all. He would advise her but at the end of the day it was another decision for her to make.

'But for now we concentrate on the surgery,' he said. 'And you will probably find more discomfort from the side effects of the anaesthetic than from the incision itself.' As I listened, I clung to the fact that Diane had a small tumour, that they had caught it so early. I tried to brush away the gnawing worry that they would find more cancer, that it had spread. I was determined to be calm and positive and strong for Diane. She seemed bright, cheerful even as she chatted to the doctor and went over things with him, asking for clarification now and again. She even made the odd joke; he never cracked a smile but the wrinkles round his eyes deepened and his eyes gleamed in appreciation. There were more forms to fill in and leaflets to take away and study. And beneath the practicality the quashed panic that gripped us both, in our different ways.

There was a new message on my office phone: a young woman with a Welsh lilt to her voice was asking me to call Piers Carruthers. For a moment, I wondered if it was a wind-up. Piers is an uncommon name and mainly reserved for landed aristocracy and the like. Coupled with Carruthers, it spoke of jolly hockey sticks and ginger ale territory. He was a lawyer. He wasn't actually at his desk when I rang but his secretary wanted to go ahead and fix an appointment with me, at his offices behind the town hall.

'Can you tell me what it's about?'

'Mr Carruthers has been appointed as legal representative to Mr Mark Florin. It's in connection with that.'

Presumably, he wanted to know what I'd gleaned while I was searching for Janet. He was a busy man but we finally settled on a meeting at six-thirty that evening.

As I drove into town a few hours later, the weather was changing. Cloud moving in from the Atlantic was smothering the sky and sealing in the heat. Summer storms were promised. The air was sticky and gritty. The pressure made my head feel thick and that, combined with my continuing unease at Janet Florin's fate, left me dizzy and nauseous. There was nowhere to park nearby so I ended up getting a space down on Deansgate and walking back to Albert Square. The neo-Gothic façade of the town hall was strung with banners celebrating Greater Manchester Youth Games. Towers of hanging baskets festooned the main entrance. The law firm was tucked away on one of the narrow lanes nearby. Carruthers and Gee, the brass doorplate stated.

Piers Carruthers wasn't your typical product of the English public school system. He was black for one thing. Afro-Caribbean descent at a guess. Before meeting him, I'd have bet fifty quid on him having a father who practised law or medicine but I'm not the betting type. I don't even do the lottery. Maddie thinks I'm mad. 'We could win, Mummy. We could be rich and have a swimming pool and a pony.' In the flesh, Piers Carruthers didn't have the cut-glass accent or effortless confidence that an upper-class background confers. He looked slightly harassed at the end of a busy day and when he spoke it was with a Geordie lilt.

We were seated in a small, shabby cluttered room with legal papers and boxes all over the place. I declined a drink as I'd been chugging water en route and I was eager to get the meeting done with and be on my way home for an early night.

Piers got straight down to business. 'I imagine you're wondering why you are here?'

Duh. 'Yes.'

'My client, Mr Florin…'

I nodded to show I was keeping up.

'…he wants to hire your services.'

'What!' I stared at the man.

'Yes. He wants me to hire you to prove his alibi.'

The same alibi I'd already trashed. I stared some more. Tried to form an appropriate response. Came up with 'Why?' I should have said 'why me?' but Piers was already speaking.

'Because he is not responsible for the death of his wife and he wants you to help furnish proof.'

I must have looked gobsmacked because he added, 'Will you at least see him before you decide?'

If I had been working for Trisha there could well have been a conflict of interest. But since Janet had been found, Trisha was no longer my client.

'Yes,' I agreed, not knowing if that was the right thing to do. Half of me wanted to run a mile but I was deeply curious. Mark Florin wanted to hire *me*. What was he playing at? 'Yes.' I nodded again. 'I'll see him.' After all, I could still walk away.

It's not unheard of for solicitors to employ private investigators to assist in gathering evidence for a case. There's a firm in Manchester, not far from Carruthers', that I do occasional work for if I'm short of clients and need some bread-and-butter income. But this was an unusual situation. It was murder for starters.

The police had been granted another twelve hours to question Mark. Rules stipulated that he be allowed to rest overnight and be given adequate meal breaks. In other words, the police wouldn't be talking to him again until the following morning. I could meet with him, in advance of that, at nine a.m.

Elizabeth Slinger police station is close to Princess Parkway, south of the city and about a mile and a half from my house. Security was tight and I had to sign in, pin on a visitor's badge, leave my bag at the front desk and pass through an X-ray scanner. They let me keep my file and notepad and pen. They too were scanned.

A constable escorted me along through two sets of security doors and into the custody suite. She took me into a small interview room and waited with me. It was a bland, over-warm box with no windows and unpleasant strip lighting. One table, three chairs and a calendar on the wall showing gardens of the world. June's picture was Durban. Though today was July 1st. No one had changed it yet. I wondered whether this was standard issue; did all the interview rooms in the GMP area have them? Or had someone based at the station brought it in thinking to cheer the place up or to re-home an unwanted Christmas gift?

When Mark Florin arrived, I was shocked at the change in his appearance. He looked smaller, his eyes had a staring, feverish cast and his skin was damp with a sweaty sheen. He smelt sour and, as the officer accompanying him indicated he should take a seat, I surreptitiously angled my chair to increase the distance between us.

What were the cells like? Bland and functional like this room, barer? Cold? Hot? More or less primitive than prison? I'd a sudden image of Berfan and Ramin, held captive. I imagined concrete blocks, iron railings, hoods and batons and dirty water.

'Give us a knock when you're done,' the policeman said. My escort tipped his head at me and the pair of them left, closing the door as they did.

I didn't waste any time on pleasantries. There was nothing very pleasant about sitting in that room with a man I thought had killed his wife.

'You want me to work for you? To prove your latest alibi?'

'That's right.' There was still a little of the old challenge in his attitude.

'I know you weren't in Liverpool; there weren't any interviews.'

'So do they,' he said flatly.

'Yes, I told them.' I wanted all the cards on the table.

He gave a sharp exhalation, cast his eyes to the side as if at some hollow joke.

'Why me?' I asked. 'Why can't the police check out your alibi? Or your solicitor?'

'The police will. But the people who can vouch for me are going to disappear if the police come asking questions. And some suit with a briefcase will have the same effect.'

'But I won't?'

'You stand more chance.'

'Where were you?'

'Liverpool.'

I held up my hand but he carried on.

'Not at Glennisters Acorn but I was in the city. I went round town for a bit, passing time. Then to a pub. Had a few. Then I picked up a couple of girls, working girls.' He stared boldly at me, daring me to react. 'Spent the afternoon with them, left coming up to four.'

'Where?'

'Some godforsaken dump near Kensington.'

'Address?'

'Don't know. We got a cab.'

'Where did you meet the girls?'

'The bar, the Anchor and Compass. One of them was there, she rang her mate when I...' he blinked, wiped his greasy forehead with one hand, 'when I said I wanted a threesome.'

'And you don't think they'll cooperate with the police?'

'I know they won't. They're not legal.'

'Underage?' I felt a kick of revulsion.

'No. Immigrants. One was African, the other's from Eastern Europe somewhere. If the police get anywhere near, they'll vanish.'

'The police haven't been yet?'

'I haven't told them all the details yet.'

'What?'

His features sharpened. 'You go first,' he insisted, 'see if they'll talk to you. My brief can give that to the police and they can check it – or try to.'

He was still playing games. Held on suspicion of murder and he still had the arrogance to think he could cherry pick information, be the judge of who was told what and when.

'Even if I could do that,' I told him, 'how much validity would hearsay from an unknown and absent witness have? If she wouldn't make an official statement and wasn't prepared to testify or be cross-examined?'

'I don't know,' he raised his voice.

I stiffened, suddenly apprised of the temper he was trying to control.

'But it's all I've fuckin' well got,' he said tightly. 'It's all I've got. Maybe the bartender will remember me. Enough bits like that can prove I was in Liverpool not in the Yorkshire Dales.'

It sounded barmy. 'I think you should tell everything to the police, explain the risk of flight of these girls and let them sort it out.'

'Why won't you help me?'

'Because I think your judgement is way out.'

He sighed again, rubbed at his face with his hands. 'If the

police go there, they'll scare them off. I'll have nothing to back me up. Sweet F. A. You might get something. There's no way they will.'

'Answer me some questions?'

'All right.'

'Did you know that Janet was having an affair?'

'Suspected. Didn't know.'

'Did you challenge her about it?'

'I didn't kill my wife.' He bit the words, his eyes blazing.

'Did you challenge her?'

'No.'

We had a staring competition for a few moments.

I looked away first.

'Any idea who the man was?'

'No.'

'You're heavily in debt.'

'Me and half the country. Look, I've had this from the police already. I didn't kill her for money, I didn't kill her for jealousy, I didn't kill her at all. She's dead and—' His mouth trembled, his Adam's apple swooped up and down. He spoke again quietly. 'I loved my wife. Some bastard... When she was missing, the kids kept asking, when's Mummy coming back? Soon, I told them, soon. They needed to hear that. I needed to say that. But she's never coming back.' He sucked his cheeks in, covered his eyes with one hand. His breathing was laboured.

It had been easy to see Mark Florin as a guilty man; my antipathy towards him had smoothed the way and his mendacity put the seal on it. But the principle of presumed innocence is something I feel passionate about. My say-so had helped put him in police custody – would I now be party to freeing him? Was he telling the whole truth this time or was this a ruse, an alibi that would be hard to verify or something he'd set up in case the police ever found Janet?

'If Mr Carruthers approves, I'll go to Liverpool today. Where's the pub? And describe the girls.'

He gave me directions to the Anchor and Compass. He told me the African girl was tall with very dark skin and braided hair; she went by the name of Poppy. The other one, Honey, was slight, she had blonde hair and tattoos around her wrists. He'd no idea whether they lived at the house they had taken him to. The afternoon had been a blur of drink and sex. He had paid half the cash upfront and Honey had gone out to score. The girls had snorted coke but he'd stuck to Scotch.

'What about the pub, the staff there?'

'The barman was balding, he wore glasses. I don't remember who else was in, a few locals, no one who stuck out.'

'Had you been there before?'

'Yes.'

'With the girls?'

'Not the same ones.'

'Often?'

'No, it's not something I'm proud of.'

Thank God for that.

'It started way back,' he went on, 'not that place but going to prostitutes. I thought when I got married it'd change.'

'She never knew?'

'No.'

* * *

When I called him, Mr Carruthers listened to my reservations about Mark holding back details of his alibi from the police but he didn't share my concern. 'We're not under any obligation to disclose this at the moment and it would be to Mr Florin's benefit if you can find witnesses who put him in a bar in Liverpool when Mrs Florin was buying petrol in the Yorkshire Dales.'

'He could have done that journey in a couple of hours, it wouldn't absolutely rule him out.'

He gave a short laugh. 'We don't need a devil's advocate. And if we can place him there within an hour or so then it virtually does exclude him. I'm happy for you to go ahead.'

'My fee? I'm aware Mr Florin has financial problems.'

'We can cover that. You have an hourly rate?'

I told him what it was. I nearly upped it a bit, as I reckoned the firm could stand it, but I'm too honest for my own good sometimes.

Back home, I called Trisha Marlowe to tell her about the state of play. I felt a responsibility to let her know what I was doing. I couldn't break confidentiality but it wasn't a secret that Mark was continuing to protest his innocence and had hired me to help in his defence.

Trisha was appalled. 'How can you do that – switch sides?'

'There are no sides, not yet.'

'The police think he killed her.' Her voice rose. 'What more do you want?'

'I want to check out the new alibi he's giving.'

'And when that turns to dust will he come up with another version? Why did he lie in the first place?'

'I can't divulge any details. You've every right to be upset but what if Mark is telling the truth? What if someone else killed Janet?'

'Benefit of the doubt?' she asked crisply.

'Yes.'

'I don't trust him, I don't like him, I never did. Why can't you just let the police do their job?'

I will. But you let me do mine, I thought to myself.

CHAPTER TWENTY

I changed my clothes so I had more chance of blending in, nothing too smart for a daytime drinking session. Ubiquitous sports T-shirt and cotton pants fit the bill for just about any everyday encounter. Packing my digital camera, a sandwich and drink and a route map, I left for Liverpool just after 10.30.

Six days earlier I'd been travelling east on the M62, up into the Pennines. Liverpool is the other direction and the journey west is less picturesque. Much of it is through low-lying farmland and old mining areas, skirting the towns of Wigan and Warrington. I saw fields of lurid rape, smallholdings with chicken coops and pigsties. Here and there, horses grazing. The mines had left traces: broken brickwork where dwellings had been, snatches of canal where the coal barges had plied their trade, scrubby landscape as nature grew over the cinders and debris of the past, carpeting it with thistles and nettles and cow parsley. A winding wheel, its struts broken and rust streaking the metal, rose petrified against the horizon. With the window down, I fancied I could smell the gassy flavour of coal on the sultry air. Coming into Liverpool was confusing, there wasn't time to follow the route map properly and I lost my way twice, having to pull into a side road and a hotel car park to get my bearings.

When I found the Anchor and Compass, I took the time to drive the length of the street and back getting a feel for my surroundings. The houses along the same side as the pub were quite large, Victorian semi-detached villas with bay windows, peeling paint and mismatched curtains. Most were multiple occupancy as evidenced by the plethora of bells and wheelie bins. One pair advertised Bed & Breakfast from £25. Further along neighbouring properties had been demolished and a small cube of maisonettes stuck in their place. Across the road, most of the housing had been torn down and replaced by prefabricated industrial units. Ventor's Packaging, close to where I parked was contained behind steel fencing and smothered in razor wire. It reminded me of Ramin's house.

In classic stranger-in-town style, all heads turned my way when I walked into the pub. There were half a dozen drinkers dotted around. All men save for a middle-aged woman who wore startling make-up like an Aunt Sally and had dyed her hair a violent puce. She had enormous breasts, set off by a black and white leopard-print top, and a slew of gold chains around her neck. The men were dowdy in comparison, a blue Everton football shirt was the brightest colour; the rest wore a variation on denims and faded T-shirts from long-ago rock band tours.

Behind the bar, holding the racing pages but studying me, sat the man Mark Florin had described. He watched unsmiling as I approached. There was no point in ordering a drink; his stance already signalled hostility and the sooner I'd said my piece the better.

'I wonder whether you can help me?'

'Doubt it,' he interrupted.

'I'm a private investigator, trying to trace this man's movements.' I showed him the picture of Mark Florin; his face now familiar to much of the British public from television and newspapers. 'He says he was drinking here three weeks ago, on the Thursday. Whisky chasers. Do you remember him?'

He shook his head slowly, his eyes flat.

Busy, were you? I resisted the temptation to say it aloud. 'He met a girl here. Poppy, a regular, I think.'

He shook his head.

'You don't mind if I ask around?'

'Free country, innit.' He made it sound anything but.

Violet leopard lady was nursing a shorts glass, its rim smeared with orange lipstick. She lit a small cigarillo as I drew closer.

'No, darling,' she answered in a nasal Liverpudlian accent as I showed her the photo and asked my questions. The knowing look in her eyes and the trace of a smirk on her mouth suggested she was lying. Perhaps putting it in context would make her reconsider. 'He's been accused of a serious crime. If he was here, he couldn't have done it.'

'I know, darling. Killed his wife, didn't he? That quarry.' She raised the cigarillo to her lips again, bangles on her arm clattered, the pungent smoke wreathed her face.

The men all said the same, either they couldn't remember or they hadn't seen him, except for one joker who may well have had a former life as a stand-up comedian on the working-men's club circuit. His nose was huge and empurpled like a knobbly sweet potato and he seemed seriously drunk.

'You chatting me up, girlie?' He raised his voice. The other drinkers shuffled in anticipation. He tapped his nose. 'What have women and dog turds got in common?'

I turned away. Saying anything would have been playing his game.

'The older they are, the easier it is to pick them up.'

Laughter hissed and cackled from several of the men. Violet leopard lady screeched with hilarity. A little too strident to be genuine.

'Naw, come 'ere, come 'ere,' he called after me. 'You wanna reliable man, don't bother with these. I could show you a good time, girlie.'

I left without looking back. Seated in the car, with a clear view of the pub, I contemplated why none of them were prepared to confirm Mark's alibi. Their reaction suggested to me that he had been there. It wasn't as if I was working for the police, trying to get someone sent down. I was trying to help an innocent man, as far as they were concerned. So why the callous disregard? Not wanting to get involved? No sense of civic responsibility?

I felt a wave of resentment towards Mark Florin. What was I doing here, waiting for a prostitute, subjecting myself to the rudeness and hostility of the pub customers, sitting cooped up in a car, growing dull with boredom? Was this all a waste of time? Was he playing me in some way that would be to his advantage?

Men from the works crossed the street to the butty bar next door to the pub. Some took their sandwiches with them into the pub to eat. I wondered what the pay was like at Ventor's Packaging. Were these skilled engineers or labourers? What did they do from nine to five? How did they cope with the repetition of clocking on day after day, seeing the same faces?

Perhaps they had good friendships, a camaraderie to make the work tolerable. Perhaps some of them even enjoyed the job.

Half an hour passed; I ate my sandwich and had a drink. Another couple of men entered the pub. The last stood out because he wore a suit. Not long after, a woman appeared. Petite and blonde, dressed in a white crop top and white miniskirt, gold espadrilles. At that distance, the tattoos on her wrists looked like bracelets. Honey. She disappeared inside the Anchor and Compass.

The wait seemed interminable. I got out of the car a couple of times to get my blood circulating again. The factory men returned to work. Then the smart chap in the suit left. A few moments later, my pulse kicked in as Honey emerged. She had arrived at the pub five minutes after the businessman and left five minutes after he did. There must be a room in the pub she can use. The regulars would all be wise to it. Their silence made more sense. The barman probably took a cut.

I heard thunder rumble off to the west, Atlantic storms had reached the Irish Sea. Honey walked along the pavement opposite. I got out of the car and locked it. She glanced at me and away quickly; they must have warned her I was snooping about. I crossed the road and blocked her path.

'Honey?'

'Do I know you?'

There was an Eastern European ring to her speech, the words formed further back in the mouth, the vowels longer, the consonants chunkier, a sibilance on the start of 'you'.

'I'm a private investigator. I have some questions—'

'No way.' She tried to walk round me.

I moved. 'A man's been accused of murder,' I told her. 'He

was with you, with you and Poppy. Your word – you can prove he didn't do it.' I showed her the picture. 'Mark Florin, he met you here. The three of you took a cab to a house. A threesome. He drank whisky.'

'Fuck off,' she said aggressively, wheeling round and walking back the way she'd come.

I followed. Her shoes slapped the pavement, her hair jounced behind her. Lightning flashed against the deep, grey clouds and thunder growled again, closer.

'Give me a statement,' I said, 'anonymously.'

Clop, clop.

'Please.'

She stopped and swung round. 'How much?'

'What?'

'How much will you pay? Must be worth a few grand.'

'I can't pay you.'

'Fuck off then.' And she stalked off.

The storm broke as I reached the outskirts of the city. The sky turned leaden grey and lightning forked in jagged neon strikes. The rain came down heavy, battering the roof of the car and making a horrific din. The wipers could barely cope with the volume of water, I had to slow my pace to have a chance of seeing ahead. By the time I reached the motorway, so much rain had fallen that I saw one car aquaplane onto the hard shoulder.

How clever was Mark? Could he have used the pub, the prostitutes, to double-bluff me and his lawyer and the police? He'd known from his previous visits that people were very unlikely to talk. But if he'd killed Janet, wouldn't he have tried to invent a better alibi? Suppose he had murdered her and then reported her missing. It would have made more sense to collect the kids and *not* officially report her gone until the next evening. That way he could engineer a solid alibi for the time of her alleged disappearance?

Imagine he sets out for Yorkshire with her. They call at the garage in Grassington. At some point after that, he hits her, fracturing her skull. He throws her into the quarry. He's late back, late picking the children up but he plays it down as a mix-up. Easily done. Ray and I have been there (well, not been there, to be precise) more than once. Mark could have then laid a trail showing how he was busy all day Friday at the leisure centre and the supermarket and the gym. All backed up by receipts and CCTV footage. He could have sent texts between his phone and hers, to make her still appear alive. That's the sort of thing you do if you want to get away with murder. If you can stay calm and clever enough to think it through. Mark's messy alibi tended to work in his favour for me. But it wasn't me that needed convincing.

CHAPTER TWENTY-ONE

'The women exist,' I told Mr Carruthers, at his office on Monday morning. 'At least, Honey does, but she's not prepared to alibi him.'

'Why on earth not?'

'Dirty washing.'

'Prostitution is hardly—'

'Illegal immigration, class A drugs. Too much to lose.'

'And the bar staff? The other customers?'

I shook my head. 'Unhelpful.'

He sighed. 'Well, the good news is the police have released Mark on bail. Not enough to charge him.'

'Are they considering someone else?'

'That's not my concern.'

'But if it helps Mark?'

'My brief is limited to my client's interests. There's no way they'll take it to trial if there's reasonable doubt.'

'It's not ideal, though.'

He laughed indulgently, shook his head as if to say such sentiments were fanciful.

'Where can I get in touch with Mark? I'd like to tell him about the trip myself.' Now I knew Mark had been released I was even more persuaded that he was an innocent man.

Piers Carruthers gave me Mark's new mobile number. The police still had his old one and wanted to retain it for examination.

Mark hadn't gone home. The press were on his tail and had been camped outside the house. His brother managed a motel and had put him up in a spare room there. It was one of those anonymous places close to motorway junctions and handy for conferences and business meetings. Budget corporate in style: bedrooms with an Internet connection, trouser press, desk and office chair, one armchair and a telly. It seemed a generous gesture until I saw that this particular room had been damaged, the ceiling light was ripped from its wiring, the walls were scuffed and marked and the door to the en suite bathroom was missing. Mark gave me the swivel chair and sat himself on the easy chair.

'So?' His face was tight with impatience.

'I found the bar, talked to the customers, met Honey. No one remembers you.'

'For God's sake.' He clutched his fists and threw back his head.

'Doesn't mean you weren't there, but they won't vouch for you.'

He put his hand to his head, pressing his thumb into his temple and his fingers into his forehead.

'Mr Carruthers sounds optimistic.'

'Oh, brilliant,' he snarled and colour flooded his face. 'No need to worry then.' A pause, then he gave a gruff, 'Sorry.'

'They have released you.'

'For now. Did Mr Carruthers also explain that they can

pick me up tomorrow or the day after and the whole bloody circus kicks off again? I'm still under suspicion. They keep going on about the debts and the life insurance.'

'But you've told them now about the alibi?' I checked.

'Yes. Not likely to get any further than you did, are they?'

'That depends. If they can trace one of the girls, she might well talk in exchange for the police ignoring other crimes. I'll speak to the police,' I added, 'tell them what I've learnt.'

That was easier said than done. Phone calls to the officer-in-charge of the inquiry were handled by other staff who were able to take down information over the phone but no more than that. They couldn't answer questions – I could have been anybody – so I couldn't find out whether any efforts had been made to visit the Anchor and Compass yet.

Fishing out the card that the big-boned DC Whittaker had left when she called at my house, just after they'd found Janet's body, I tried her next. They put me on hold, then transferred me a couple of times. I was losing patience when she finally came on the line. She sounded weary and I'd a glimpse of her still in the same crumpled linen suit. Once she'd grasped what I was on about, her tone sharpened. She was at my house within half an hour. Linen suit an' all.

She was furious. This time there were none of the brisk smiles. She was probably younger than me but in her controlled disapproval managed to make me feel like I'd been summoned to the head teacher's office.

'You tried to verify a suspect's alibi? A suspect in a murder inquiry?'

'His lawyer knew about it.'

She snorted.

Digger scrambled to his feet and trotted into the hall, then I heard the door. Ray and the kids were back from school.

'We'll need a full statement. If you'll accompany me to the station.'

The kids ran in and Tom slung his bag on the table and stared curiously at DC Whittaker.

Forestalling comments, as Ray walked into the kitchen, I said, 'This is someone from work. We're off to a meeting. I've got my mobile.'

Ray picked up on the atmosphere and followed us into the hall. 'Everything OK?' he asked me.

'Fine.' Though I felt nervy inside.

'How long are you going to be?'

I looked at Whittaker.

'Hard to say,' she replied.

There was no chitchat en route and when we arrived at the police station I was treated with cold politeness.

Sitting in the same interview room as I'd met Mark Florin in, with its floral celebration of Durban on the wall, DC Whittaker and DC Tan, her partner, questioned me in laboured detail about my Liverpool trip. They wanted descriptions of the customers, verbatim details about the questions I'd asked and the answers given. They did not want my suppositions and certainly not my suggestions. When I ventured the notion that the girls were reputed to be living here illegally, Whittaker gave an irritable blink of her eyes and a little sigh.

We went over events again and DC Tan laboriously wrote out a statement which I signed.

By then I was famished. I hadn't eaten since lunchtime and my back ached from holding myself rigid with apprehension. I wanted food and a hot bath. I wanted to go home. Half rising, I began to say my goodbyes but DC Whittaker cut across me. 'A few more questions, Miss Kilkenny.'

I sat back down.

'You told us you were working for Trisha Marlowe.'

It sounded like an accusation. 'I was and then Janet was found.'

'And who are you working for now?'

'Mark Florin. And his solicitor.'

'When did you start working for Mr Florin?'

'Just this morning, well – last night.'

'Did you know him before?'

'Before what?'

'Before Trisha Marlowe hired you?'

'No.'

'Had you met him before?'

'No.'

'Did you inform Mr Florin that his wife was having an affair?'

Whittaker's face was set, she leant in towards me, her bulk intimidating.

'No, I, erm...' I stumbled over my words, trying to get clear the sequence of events. 'No, I asked Mr Florin if his wife was seeing anyone else. He said he suspected she was.' I recalled his comment about the sex being different.

'He was suspicious?' DC Tan asked. 'Did you find anything that substantiated this?'

I reminded them about the bogus yoga class.

'And you told Mr Florin about this?' Whittaker asked.

'No, I was working for Trisha Marlowe at that point.'

'But now you are working for him?'

'We've not talked about Janet, he wants me to corroborate his movements, that's all.'

They kept on in a similar vein. The subtext was that I was colluding with Mark Florin in some way. It was never stated openly so I couldn't refute it but it hovered like a distasteful smell.

'If Mark Florin didn't kill Janet then someone else did,' I pointed out.

Whittaker looked at me as if I was stupid. Again, she ignored the comment. I'd had enough. 'Can I leave now?'

'Certainly.' She pushed her chair back and rose. 'Leave the police work to us from now on,' she said coldly. 'Your intervention hasn't done your client any favours. And you may well have prejudiced our inquiries. If that is the case you could face charges.'

The reprimand stung. I wanted to justify my actions but I wanted to get away from there even more.

I didn't bother to say goodbye.

In the taxi home, gazing out at the rain-washed streets, I ran through the arguments in my head: Florin's lawyer was happy hiring me; Mark was sure the police wouldn't get within spitting distance when they tried; he trusted me to do better. But in all honesty, a small part of me feared that my actions had made it harder for the police to verify his story. Once Honey and Poppy had been alerted by me, wouldn't they just disappear? There's still the bartender, I reassured myself, and the customers. Even if the girls went to ground, those regulars would be there looking for company and oblivion in the steady chug of alcohol through the long afternoons. It only needed one of them to give the police a nod and Mark would be in the clear.

CHAPTER TWENTY-TWO

On the way back from school the following morning, I got a text from Diane. 'U busy?'

I replied that I'd be there soon. When she opened the door, she looked woebegone: her face puffy and streaked with tears, her eyes watery and bloodshot. I didn't say anything, just stepped inside and hugged her. She gave a little shudder. It reminded me of the aftermath of Maddie's crying jags when the tears have gone but the dry sobs continue, her narrow shoulders jerking up and down.

'Bad day?'

She moved away and I followed her into the kitchen.

'Jesus!' Everything was smashed. The floor was awash with broken china and glass. Plates, cups, bowls, food jars and bottles, flour canisters, cookie jars. Everything that she kept on her shelves. There was a smell of brine and vinegar.

'What happened?' A break-in? Local scallies amusing themselves?

'I got angry,' she said. 'I got so angry.'

'So I see. Good job you did the baking first or you'd have been buggered.' I looked at her and saw the glint of humour flare in her eyes. She began to laugh. It was infectious and the pair of us cackled and chortled and hooted until we were short of breath and red-faced.

'It's OK,' she told me, 'part of the process.'

'Got any bin liners?'

We doubled them up and shovelled in the shards of pottery and glass and the debris. Then swept and mopped the floor.

'Have you anything left to drink out of?'

'Some old bits in here.' She stooped to a corner cupboard brought out a plain brown mug with a chip in it. She rooted around some more and held up a squat cup with a picture of a field mouse painted on the side. 'Tea?'

'Coffee?' I asked.

'Gone.'

'I'll get some. And milk.'

At the corner shop I bought a jar of overpriced instant and a pint carton of semi-skimmed.

We sat and drank coffee and chatted until I was sure she was OK to be left on her own. Pausing on the doorstep, I told her, 'Thanks for texting me.' She nodded. We both knew it was a milestone, a marker that Diane would ask for help if she needed it and not be too proud or stubborn to do so.

Late afternoon, I got a call. A woman's voice with a Scouse twang. 'May I speak to Sal Kilkenny, please?'

For a delirious moment, I imagined it was someone calling about Mark Florin's alibi.

'Speaking.'

'This is Lily Shen. You came to school – you asked us about Janet.'

'Yes.' I remembered Lily, Janet's teaching assistant.

'I can't believe what's happened. That she's been murdered. How could anyone do that?'

A rhetorical question. Why was Lily ringing? Did she think I might know something more?

But then she went on to say. 'I remembered something but I don't know if it's important or not. Can I come and see you?'

'Where are you?'

'In Reddish. But there's plenty of buses.'

'I can drive,' I told her. 'Just give me the address.'

Picture a working-class district in a northern mill town. Small red-brick terraced houses running in rows out from the looming mill and its towering chimney. A shop on every other corner, and here and there a church or school built in the same garish red brick, perhaps with a bit of cream stonework for contrast. Update it by closing the mill and converting it into bargain factory outlets selling mirrors, foam cut to size, beds and uPVC windows. Add in satellite dishes and cars parked along the roadsides, as none of the houses have off-road parking or garages, and you get a notion of Reddish.

Lily's front door opened straight into an open-plan living room. Stairs ran up one wall, a tiny, gleaming kitchen took up the far end of the space and the rest was dominated by a black leather sofa and a TV. A couple of framed photos hung on the wall where once there would have been a fireplace. One featured the New York skyline, the other a similar study of Liverpool Pier Head. I guessed Lily had grown up in Liverpool, going by her accent. The picture showed the Three Graces all built in white stone: the Liver building with its twin pinnacles, a bird on top of each; the full square block of the Cunard building and the domed roof of the old Docks and Harbour Offices.

I declined her offer of a drink and sat down. Lily's face was solemn, her look pensive. She clasped her hands together, rested them on her knees, preparing to explain.

'There was this man Janet talked about.'

My pulse perked up. The mystery lover?

'She'd been working with him at another school before she came to ours.'

'A teacher?' I asked.

Lily nodded. 'The deputy head. Janet suspected him of siphoning off money from some of the school funds. She wasn't sure whether to tell anybody – it wasn't like she could prove it.'

'Why did she suspect him? Wouldn't something like that show up in an audit, wouldn't the governors see there was money missing?'

· Lily spread her palms. 'I don't know. There's always a way, isn't there? Fiddling petty cash, using a capital budget to slide money sideways, claiming for things that have gone missing in break-ins when maybe they haven't, whatever.'

I was surprised at her grasp of financial scams. She noticed and laughed. 'Eh, look,' she said, 'when you're on a TA's wage you dream up all sorts of ways to make money. Most of 'em illegal.'

'Did Janet report him?'

'No. I never thought about it until I heard, you know...when you came to school, you were just asking how she'd been, like whether she was seeing anyone. But now I'm wondering whether I should tell the police.'

'I think you should, yes. They can decide whether it's relevant. Though if she never took any action, then it seems very unlikely this man would harm her.'

She nodded slowly and blew a little sigh through her lips.

'What was he called?' I asked her.

'Tennant. He's at Mersey High.'

'When Janet told you about him – how did it come up?'

Lily concentrated, hands clasped again. 'We were probably just having a moan about things,' she concluded. 'I don't really remember.'

As I drove back through the relentless urban sprawl, negotiating the life-threatening mega-roundabouts that the borough of Stockport seems to revel in constructing, I considered Lily's account.

Had Janet decided to act? Had she made a move against Mr Tennant? If so, would the threat of exposure be enough to drive him to kill her? And if it was him, how on earth had he persuaded her into his car for a trip to the Dales? If she'd been with him under duress, he'd hardly have let her out to pay for the petrol in Grassington. He wouldn't have given her the chance to escape or ask for help. Could she have been blackmailing him? Janet and Mark were struggling financially; putting the squeeze on Mr Tennant might have brought some money in. But there was no sign of that in their bank accounts. Besides, that still didn't explain why she would be with him in Yorkshire.

Maybe it wasn't him? He could have hired someone to silence her. A hit-man. OK – fantastical, but it's not unheard of. If Janet's actions led to his conviction for fraud, he'd lose his job and his status and possibly serve time in jail. Worth killing for?

* * *

What would Trisha Marlowe's take on the Oliver Tennant business be? I called her.

'Awful man,' she said, when I asked her about him. Then she paused and her voice became crisper. 'You don't think he—'

'I don't know. It's just he's the closest thing I've found to an enemy. Someone who could have posed a threat. What did Janet say about him?'

'She really hated him. She thought he was committing some sort of fraud but she was only a supply teacher, she had no security in that job. She didn't feel she could say anything.' Trisha gave an exasperated sigh. 'People like that get away with—oh, God.' She broke off, unseated by the now sinister resonance of the well-worn phrase.

Like many schools nowadays, Mersey High has a website. It was a stylish, well-designed site with lots of photographs and graphics. Oliver Tennant was listed as the deputy principal and there was a thumbnail photo, too. I clicked on this and studied the larger image. He was older than I'd expected, with a stiff, white moustache, short white hair and old-fashioned wire-rimmed glasses.

Lifting the phone book down from the top of my filing cabinet, I checked the entries. 'O' is an unusual initial and there was only one O. Tennant listed. It had been easy to find him, and his address.

So what was I going to do? Call him? Turn up at the house? Pointing the finger at a possible murder suspect didn't seem like a sensible step to take but maybe I could get some information from Mrs Tennant, instead. If there was one.

* * *

First thing the next day, I rang the school, asked to speak to Mr Tennant and was told he was in a meeting. No, I didn't want to leave a message. Enough to know he was safely out of the way.

The Tennant house was a lovely old villa, a couple of steps up the scale from the Victorian semi we live in. This must have had six or seven bedrooms, acres of stained glass and Tudor trim, a coach house and gardens to die for. Well, potentially. The Tennant's grounds consisted of an expanse of lawn and borders colonised by rhododendrons with dense yew trees around the perimeter. The shrubs were now so large and dominant that the whole scheme was an unremitting bottle green. Sure, they'd look stunning in full flower but what about the other ten months of the year? And nothing would grow beneath them; rhododendrons poison the soil.

I crunched my way up the gravel drive and rang the brass doorbell. The exterior of the house was in immaculate condition. It must cost a fortune in upkeep. Reason perhaps for creaming off the school funds – if indeed he had. But maybe the Tennants had independent means. I wasn't even sure what a deputy head would earn: 50k, 60k? Maybe Mrs T. had a well-paid job, too.

The first thing that struck me when she opened the door was how terribly thin she was. Her hair was dyed a sort of minky blonde, styled in a stiff, helmet shape. She had a sharp face, emphasised by specs that swept upwards like cat's eyes. Her cheekbones jutted out and it looked as though someone had scooped away the flesh beneath them. Her skin was pale and lightly freckled. She wore a short-sleeved, roll-neck top, knitted in a fine grey wool and tailored grey trousers. She held a cigarette in one scraggy, blue-veined hand.

'Mrs Tennant?' I asked.

'Yes?'

I held out my card. 'I'm working privately for Mark Florin. His wife—'

'His wife was a nasty piece of work. Threatening to drag a decent man's name through the dirt. Making false allegations.'

'Hang on.'

She ignored me and carried on at full throttle. 'Accusing others of wrong-doing when she was nothing short of a trollop herself.'

'How do you mean?'

'Look it up – it's in the dictionary. You can read?'

'Listen, I—'

'She was cheating on her husband. Didn't want that getting out, did she? She soon stopped her slanderous innuendo when faced with that. Had her own dirty little secret, didn't she?' She took a suck on the cigarette, swallowed the smoke hungrily.

'How do you know?'

'I saw them,' she breathed out smoke, 'checking into a hotel in Buxton. Now, I'd like you to go.' She tapped the ash off the end of her cigarette.

'Can you describe him, do you know who it was?'

'No. If you don't leave now, I'll call the police. I'll press charges.'

'The police would be very interested, I'm sure. Which hotel?'

'Now!'

She wasn't kidding. I crunched my way back down the drive, feeling frustrated. This was the first person I'd talked to who had tangible proof that Janet was involved with someone, who could help identify him.

According to Mrs Tennant, Janet *had* confronted Oliver Tennant about her concerns. Though Janet hadn't told Lily that, or Trisha. She couldn't – otherwise, she would have to explain the hold that Tennant had over her: that he knew about her adultery. He bought her silence, blackmailed her into keeping quiet. Had it worked? Or had she gone ahead, defied him and set out to raise it with someone. And had he then used a more permanent method of silencing her?

As I reached the car, my phone rang. It was Ramin. 'Berfan is missing again,' he said urgently. 'He leave the hospital.'

I went round to the house. We sat in the little kitchen with its posters and plastic chairs while he told me what he knew. Two other men, looking subdued, followed our conversation but didn't say anything.

'He ran from the nurse and got out of the fire exit.'

'When?'

'In the night.'

'Where would he go?'

'I don't know,' said Ramin softly. 'They want to see me at the hospital.'

'I'll take you.'

'Thank you.'

Doctor Akstan seemed to think Ramin could tell her where Berfan would head for, but we explained that there wasn't anywhere obvious.

'How was he dressed?' I asked her. 'Did he have shoes on?'

'Yes.'

'How was he yesterday? Was he upset? Had you any idea he was planning to run away?'

She hesitated. 'I didn't see him yesterday. None of the nursing staff raised any concerns.' There was a caution in her manner, a sense of holding back and it struck me that she was thinking about the institution and how best to protect it, rather than thinking about Berfan. That made me hanker for an apology of sorts, some admission that they'd failed to provide the best possible care for him. Not for purposes of litigation or blame or anything but simply as an act of humanity. Ramin was extremely worried.

'This is awful.' I looked at her directly.

'He isn't dangerous,' she said.

'He isn't safe,' I countered.

CHAPTER TWENTY-THREE

These were twitchy times, in the aftermath of the London bombings, and a young man of Asian or Arabic appearance acting stressed could find himself suspected of being a terrorist. If anyone challenged Berfan, I guessed his instinct would be to run, so inviting hostile fire. I reined in my imagination as we left the hospital and tried to focus on anything practical we could do. The police had Berfan's details and would return him to the hospital if apprehended.

'Has he any money?' I asked Ramin.

'A little. I left him some for sweets and cigarettes.'

'Not enough to travel very far, then?'

The only thing I could think of was to try the places Berfan knew: the Welcome Centre, Piccadilly Gardens. If he was confused and frightened perhaps somewhere like that, a familiar place, would appeal to him. What else could we do?

It was a miserable task. At the Welcome Centre, no one we asked had seen Berfan or heard anything of him. Ramin looked shattered, his face was drained and that accentuated the pitted texture of his skin. I suggested we stop and take a break, get a cup of coffee but he shook his head. He wanted to be out there, doing something.

By the time we got to Piccadilly Gardens, I'd decided this truly was a hopeless quest. We trudged round the square, walked down Market Street and back then sat for a minute on one of the park benches. I looked across to the fountains where two toddlers were tottering about.

'I don't know what else we can do,' I said.

Ramin wrapped his arms tight across his chest. He leant forward as though he was cold and began to speak. 'When they first come you are fearful,' his voice was soft. 'You try and be—' He halted. 'The pain.' He sucked in a breath, shook his head. His heels were raised, his knees were juddering up and down. 'They want names. Who is your ally, who is planning with you? You give them names.'

There was a pause. It stretched out. I watched the little children playing, one of them clapping his hands with glee. A flock of pigeons took off at the sound, flew in an arc above the high roofs opposite.

'I give them my little brother,' Ramin said. 'I give them Berfan.'

'Oh, Ramin, I'm sorry.'

'He nearly died. He don't talk. They break his feet, his...' Ramin pushed at his own chest, '...lung. They lash him.'

'The scars.'

'Scars everywhere. Now in his mind. They are still killing him. I put him there, in prison.' Contempt distorted his expression.

'No,' I said, struggling for words to reassure him. 'They know people will talk, that's how it works, isn't it?' I glanced at him. 'Does Berfan know?'

'Oh, yes. They tell him, another stick to beat him. He

forgives me.' There was anguish as he spoke. Ramin had not forgiven himself.

'How can they send him back?' I wondered.

'They say it is safe now,' he replied.

'Is it, for him, for you?'

'I don't want to go back. Most of my family is gone. Very bad times.'

After a few moments, I broke the silence. 'I'll take you home.'

I was manoeuvring the car down the steep ramps on the way out of the car park, when Ramin's phone rang. He started, fumbling for it in his jeans pocket. He listened for a second then spoke. 'Berfan? Berfan?' Ramin's voice rose. He said something, repeated it. Then another phrase, his tone stricken. He hit his own head, slammed the phone, still gripped in his fist, onto his leg.

'What? Where is he, what did he say?'

'I keep asking him. By the motorway, is all he will say.'

Motorway got us nowhere. Manchester's choked by them.

'Then why did he call?' I pulled over and parked outside a church.

'He say goodbye, he has to go.'

'Go where?'

Ramin put his hands to his face. 'I don't know. We have to find him.'

'How? There are miles of motorway: the M60, M56, 61, 62.'

'It was noisy.'

A big help. 'Traffic noise?'

'Yes. But...' he scowled. 'There was noise from a truck, HGV. Beep, beep, beep'

Had he lost it? I tried to follow. A truck – beep, beep, beep. 'Reversing! Backwards? Yes?'

Ramin nodded.

'He wasn't on the motorway, then,' I said. 'You can't reverse on the motorway itself. But if he was at the motorway services. Using a payphone...'

'I think this is right,' Ramin's face came alive with intensity.

The road atlas was in the boot. The nearest motorway services to the hospital where Berfan had been held were at Knutsford where the M56 joined the M6. Twenty minutes away. Was that the right one? Would he still be there? He might have hitched a lift and be miles away already.

Ramin was wound up like a spring beside me and I drove as quickly as was safe. The petrol gauge was creeping into the red but I prayed it would last. When we reached the services, I drove around the car park and the lorry park to see if there was any sign of Berfan. Nothing. I parked up and on foot we scoured the café and the shop. With lots of travellers milling about, scanning the crowds was like trying to count ripples. My hopes for finding him receded the longer we looked. He must have travelled further, or be on another route. He could have been ringing from a business park close to a motorway, somewhere by the M60 ring road, perhaps. Maybe the motorway claim had been a lie to send Ramin in the wrong direction. But then why ring at all? We went outside and circled the car park on foot again. No sign.

I grabbed Ramin by the arm and he recoiled. A cultural

thing, probably. I withdrew my hand and asked him about their conversation. 'When Berfan said he had to go, was it like he was in a hurry, getting a lift perhaps? He could have hitch-hiked out of here while we were on our way.'

Ramin shook his head disconsolately. 'Maybe,' he said.

Or was it a different sort of goodbye? Perhaps Berfan didn't expect to see his brother again. He was giving up, giving in to his demons.

'There'll be security around here, somewhere. We should find them, ask for help.'

Before Ramin could reply, the sound of an altercation reached us from the exit of the lorry park at the far side of the area. We began to run without even consulting each other. Voices came from the front of a large HGV, which had stopped diagonally across the roadway at an angle to another wagon, a tanker. The lorry's door was open, its engine thundering away.

As we reached the front of the vehicle, we saw Berfan a few yards ahead. Relief flooded my veins. A large, irate man in shorts and vest top and muddy tattoos pushed Berfan in the chest then wheeled away. Two other men were shouting at Berfan.

'You want fucking locking up.'

'Tosser.'

'Bloody lunatic,' the vest guy said. Incandescent with rage he turned to bear down on Berfan again.

Ramin called to his brother. We closed the gap quickly. Berfan winced as the man pushed him again. Ramin shouted at him to stop.

I yelled at the two other men. 'What's going on?'

The bloke in the vest whirled round to face us. 'That nutter,' he jabbed a finger at Berfan, 'ran in front of my rig. I missed him.' He held up his hand, a thick finger and thumb measuring a hair's breadth. 'That close!' The man's aggression was born of the anger and adrenalin that the near collision had aroused. The same reaction that propels some parents, who earlier were manically searching for their missing children, to lash out at them once they know they are safe.

'Get the police,' one of the onlookers yelled.

'It's all right,' I said. 'We'll take him, we've been looking for him.'

Ramin was pulling at Berfan, trying to move him away from the animosity of the men but Berfan, who had a feverish expression, was resisting.

'It's not all right. Not by a long chalk. He wants charging with reckless endangerment. Not just himself he might have killed. I had to swerve. If I'd gone into that,' he pointed to the tanker, 'it'd have been a fucking disaster.'

'Sorry,' Ramin said. 'Sorry, sorry.' He dragged Berfan, his arms around his chest. I saw that there were bloody grazes on Berfan's elbows and all along the undersides of his arms.

'Maybe that's what he wanted,' the other bystander said.

There was sudden silence as the prospect of a terrorist trying to cause a chemical explosion dangled before us.

'He's ill.' I spoke up. 'We're taking him with us.'

The vest man shook his head. I felt sorry for him. His outrage was perfectly understandable, he was badly shaken by the accident. There were grunts and murmured comments but no one prevented us from leaving.

* * *

I had some water in the car and a couple of apples.

'Sit him in the back, see if he'll have some,' I told Ramin. His brother refused the fruit but he did take a mouthful of water. He was grubby, his lips were cracked and red. He acted as though I wasn't there, not responding to anything I said, or even looking my way. His limbs twitched, from fright perhaps or a symptom of his illness or medication. The sooner he was back in the hospital, the better. I rang their number and explained the situation, told them exactly where we were. We needed someone to come and restrain Berfan, get him back there safely.

'Ramin, has he got his medicine with him?'

Ramin asked but Berfan ignored him. He was muttering.

'What's he saying?'

'He is praying.'

Ramin began to talk over him. By his tone, I judged he was trying to calm him down, reassure him. It didn't have much impact. Berfan trembled violently, his head bobbing back and forth, his legs shuddering.

With no idea how long help would take to arrive, I was eager to find someone closer at hand to assist us, transport police or security guards. Reluctant to leave Ramin with Berfan, I began to suggest that we went together to the main building when there was a sudden movement from the back seat and Berfan flung open his door. Ramin lunged after him, his fist closing on thin air. He and I clambered out of the car at the same time. Ramin was yelling Berfan's name.

Berfan hared away between the parked cars. We raced after him. I willed myself to increase my speed, feeling my muscles tighten at the sudden spurt I put on. Gulping breaths of warm air, I still couldn't close the distance between us.

Berfan swerved to the right towards the petrol station. Ramin was ahead of me when a reversing car forced him to run wide.

As the forecourt came into sight, I saw Berfan by one of the pumps, clutching the hose. Liquid spilling out. Over his head. Then Ramin slammed into him, tried wresting the hose from him.

There was a volley of shouts.

'Eh, what the fuck?' Someone swore.

'What do they think—'

I'd almost reached them, flying past the shocked and bewildered faces of motorists, when Berfan wrenched away from Ramin and careered off, his hair and arms shiny with fuel. Ramin in pursuit, slipped, scrambled to his feet and pelted after him. Berfan stopped at the edge of the forecourt. He put his hand in his pocket, withdrew it and flicked with his thumb. The spark from the lighter caught the vapour and a sheet of flame ignited over Berfan's upper body. Berfan twisted and staggered, a pillar of fire. Ramin flew to him, knocking him over and smothering the flames in an embrace.

By the time I reached them, the fire was out. The air reeked with the oily stink of petrol and the sulphuric stench of burnt hair. Berfan was twitching. His head and chest were blackened and crinkled, his T-shirt melted and charred. In a couple of places, his skin had split to reveal angry, raw flesh beneath. Ramin, kneeling beside him, had burns along his arms and one side of his face; his clothes were scorched. Black flakes floated in the sunshine. Sirens wailed. Berfan stopped moving. He was dead. He looked tiny, lying there, like a boy.

Ramin fell upon him again, calling out. Then he sat back on his heels, lifted his face to the sky and cried out again and again, slapping at his own cheeks and his chest.

CHAPTER TWENTY-FOUR

The blessing of shock sealed me off from the next few hours as we were assessed by paramedics, taken to hospital, questioned by police officers. I recall only small details: my teeth chattering though the day was warm; the surreality of watching the incident as 'breaking news' on television as I waited in casualty; becoming confused about getting my car back and flashbacks not only to Berfan's death but to a house fire I'd been in, where a young man and a small child had lost their lives.

They agreed to let me go home if someone I knew could take me back and keep an eye on me. The police had explained that my car remained part of a crime scene and would be examined in the investigation into Berfan's death. Although many people had witnessed the suicide, there had to be a coroner's inquest. Ramin had been transferred to the burns unit. They wouldn't let me see him, he'd been sedated and they didn't want him disturbed.

Ray was at work. When I rang him, he wasted no time in coming to get me. I felt grimy and heartsick and shaky by then. The horror of what had happened lodged in the core of me. Sitting in a plastic bucket chair in the waiting area, I sipped at water and let the ebb and flow of fresh emergencies arriving, the sound of ambulance sirens dying on the wind, wash over me.

'Sal.'

He was there: kneeling in front of me. Hands cupping my head, eyes searching mine. I couldn't talk, my eyes stung, my mouth tremored. He stood, placed one hand under my elbow. 'Come on.' He walked me to his car, one arm around my shoulders, holding onto me, holding me up. Walking in his embrace, like lovers do. Something we'd never done before. So many things we'd never done. Hadn't done yet. So little time.

The need to talk about Berfan's death was overwhelming. 'He was so quick,' I told Ray as we travelled home. 'He ran so fast. One minute he was in the car and then—'

'They say he was ill.'

'Yes.' I told Ray the whole story from the moment I'd first met Ramin with Rachel in the supermarket and they'd asked me to look for his brother.

'He'd already run in front of a lorry. We should have held him down. Tied his ankles up or something.'

'You weren't to know. If he was set on it.'

'He was only twenty-two. He'd been tortured in Iran. What sort of world is it, Ray?'

He didn't answer for long enough. I gazed out at the houses slipping by, the trees in all their greens from mint, to teal, to deepest emerald, the pylons. The people getting in and out of cars, carrying shopping, pushing strollers and walking dogs. Untouched by today.

I heard the intake of his breath, the little snick as he parted his lips to speak. 'I love you, Sal.'

He made me cry.

* * *

Ray had arranged for Tom and Maddie to go to friends overnight. An unexpected treat for a school day. When we got back, he took round their night things. It was a wise arrangement. In the shadow of the trauma, I'd an urge to gather everything precious to me close and hold on tight but I didn't trust my emotions and I didn't want to subject the kids to the sight of me ranting or bawling. It would have been different if someone they knew had died but at the end of the day this was work and my burden.

While he was out, I showered, trying to get rid of the smell of petrol and the sweat and grime. I made a huge mug of milky coffee and a honey and banana sandwich on multi-grain bread. Digger watched me eat, his eyes tracing the movement of hand to mouth, yearning for a morsel. His diligence paid off – I fed him the crusts.

The intense adrenalin had leaked away with my tears and I was bone-tired. My back and limbs ached as though I'd been pummelled. All I wanted to do was close my eyes. Upstairs, I lay down on my bed and pulled the covers over me. Consciousness loosened its grip and I was falling into oblivion like a stone.

When I woke, disoriented, it was early evening, the sky awash with licks of peach and indigo across electric blue. The house was silent. I didn't want to be alone. Ray was downstairs sitting at the kitchen table. He'd just finished eating. The smell made my mouth water.

'You hungry?' He asked.

'Takeaway?'

'Veg biryani and rice.'

'Yes.'

He got up and put my meal in the microwave. I got out cutlery and a plate. Digger whined. 'I'll take him out,' Ray said.

The food was delicious, subtly spiced, the vegetables still firm, the rice flavoured with clove and cardamom. I cleared away and waited for Ray to get back. Normally self-reliant, happy with my own company, I wanted to be wrapped up in his.

The phone rang and my first thought was that Maddie hadn't settled or had forgotten something she needed for school.

'Hello?'

'Sal Kilkenny?'

'Yes.'

'Chris Lorgen here, *Independent News*. I believe you witnessed the self-immolation of an Iranian asylum seeker, earlier today. Could you spare a few moments—'

'No,' I interrupted. 'No. I can't. Sorry.' I hung up, my pulse racing and switched the phone to answer mode. The prospect of talking about what had happened, to a stranger looking for quotes, appalled me.

Ray arrived back bearing bottles of wine. He held one up.

'I'd love some,' I told him.

He filled two large glasses and waved towards the lounge.

'Some day, eh?' he said as we settled on the sofa.

Sighing, I took a big drink, then another. The wine was South African, heavy and plummy in my mouth. I swallowed and soon felt it loosen the back of my neck.

'And now this.' I gestured to him and me – the situation, the quiet room.

'You don't think you should try and relax?'

I considered how to explain. 'It's like everything's stopped. The panic and then the forms and procedures and authorities. Like a freeze frame.'

'The phone was going mad earlier.'

'Was it?'

'Probably all start up again tomorrow.'

'I don't want to talk to anyone,' I said quickly.

He held up his hands. 'Fine, fine.' He picked up the bottle.

'You trying to get me drunk?'

'Yep.' He smiled. Like a light coming on. I felt a surge of affection. Held out my glass.

We shared trivia, swapped stories of worst hangovers, deadliest drink combinations (mine was cherry B and Guinness), worst drunken decisions. I got giddy and a fit of the giggles gave me hiccups. When we'd finished the wine, I was still hiccuping, sounding like a frog. I tried to kiss him but the croaking made it impossible.

He stopped laughing, studied me carefully. 'You tired?'

I knew what he was asking. 'No.' Hunger for him swept through me. Suddenly sober, serious.

'Be right back.'

He returned in minutes, damp from the shower, a towel round his waist.

I swallowed, stood to meet him. Felt his kisses on my throat and my shoulders, his hands easing off my blouse and pants. His hands warm and strong on my waist, stroking my belly, cupping my breasts.

It was all I wanted. 'Please.' I couldn't wait, eager to feel the fit of our bodies, hot and taut. He met my mood. Our lovemaking was fast and fierce and brazen. He encouraging me with his breathless words, chanting my name. He watched me as I came, drinking in my abandon and using it to drive his own climax.

Entangled together, his sweat cooling on my skin, I listened to his heartbeat, feeling it reverberate though my body as it gradually slowed.

He nudged me and we made it upstairs, crawled into my bed together. I fell asleep in his arms. Hiccups gone, nightmares at bay. Lost and found.

CHAPTER TWENTY-FIVE

Nightmares forced me from my bed in the early hours. I promised myself that I'd go see a counsellor. There was someone I'd been to previously who had helped me to regain my equilibrium. I'd go back to her.

Awake, but lacking the ability to relax with a good book, I crept downstairs, made a drink and sat in the kids' playroom at the front of the house waiting for dawn to break. The milky light stole across the sky, the birds were muttering and squabbling. Then the sun, fat and yolky yellow climbed over the rooftops and swiftly up, shrinking as it did. The sky blazed summer blue and the first planes made their mark, early flights to summer sun. People making the most of the prices before the school holidays sent them soaring.

I couldn't settle. Wanting air, I went round to my office to get the post. The sun streamed through the low window and I angled my chair so the heat fell on my back. In the bundle of papers, there was a swathe of loan offers, two different switch energy-supplier leaflets and a note from Bob Swithinbank. He thanked me for the photos from Sandra and enclosed a cheque. He'd paid for more time than the visit to Sandra's had taken. It was a kind gesture. I decided to keep half and send the rest to Rachel's refugee charity.

I rang the hospital from there and they told me that Ramin was comfortable but was still sedated and was not permitted visitors yet. I put the phone down and felt my knees weaken, my back shiver. Sitting at my desk, I thought about the sequence of events, tried to explain to myself what had happened. Not by examining the flickering images of the tragedy or recalling the smell or the sound of shouts when we first found Berfan but by trying to simplify events into a few short sentences.

Berfan had been imprisoned and tortured in Iran. He'd fled to the UK with Ramin. The brothers had applied for asylum and Berfan's request had been denied. He became mentally ill and was sectioned. He ran away from hospital. He was suicidal. He ran in front of a truck. Then he set himself on fire. No mystery.

Would it have made any difference if his application had been granted? He'd probably been suffering from post-traumatic stress since his persecution. Was it inevitable that his mental health would deteriorate so dramatically? Should I have acted differently? If I'd called the police when we first headed for the motorway services, would they have come? On the off-chance we might find him there. Or if I had sought out the security office as soon as we'd reached the place, enlisted their help, would things have been any better?

I lay my head on my arms and closed my eyes and stayed there until my limbs grew stiff and my hands got numb.

When Maddie came home, I felt a rush of joy and an undertow of grief. I was so lucky, she was so precious and being close to death made me savour life. It was a lesson I'd learnt before but it's easy to get lazy and let the perspective slip away. Maddie was in a bad temper. She'd fallen out with her best friend and didn't want to go to her house or stupid school anymore. I checked out it was just a tiff; Maddie had been both bullied and bully before then, and I was super-sensitive to anything like that coming up.

'Sounds like you need cheering up.'

'And me.' Tom was eager to be in on any treats.

'Come on then.' I refused to tell them where we were going. Set off walking.

Five minutes later, Maddie grumbled, 'It won't cheer me up if my legs drop off.'

'Nearly there.'

We were on the edge of Didsbury village. I steered them into Caffè Uno.

'We having some tea?' Tom asked.

'Just pudding.'

'Yesss!' Maddie's eyes lit up.

They ordered double chocolate knickerbockers and I had coffee and death by chocolate. I'm pretty strict about sweets and generally limit them to mealtimes and special occasions so this was licence indeed. Maddie struggled to finish hers but the walk back would settle her indulgence. If I'd been driving, I'm sure she'd have thrown up.

My chocolate dessert was divine: silky, sweet with a bitter tang and the musky note of the best cocoa. Perfect with the rich coffee. For a while, I felt close to normal. It was a delusion.

They let me see Ramin the next day. He was in a four-bed ward, the curtains drawn around each bed. There were signs everywhere about germs, notices telling nurses to wash their hands after every contact with patients and posters stating that flowers were forbidden due to the risk of infection and contamination.

Ramin's wounds were covered with shiny gel and some with burn dressings. He barely spoke as I told him how sorry I was and asked if I could help him. I was there for ten minutes feeling increasingly uncomfortable. Probably, I reminded him of the whole terrible mess: I was part of the combination of circumstances that led to his brother's suicide. He looked at me twice in all the time I was there. Once when I arrived, when I thought I caught an expression of defeat in his gaze, and again, when, just before leaving, I said, 'You did everything you could for Berfan, all you could.' He glanced at me and his eyes flared, with pain or perhaps anger. I thought he'd speak but he turned away and closed in on himself again.

I was crossing the hospital car park, heading for the bus, when someone called my name. It was my friend Rachel, the social worker who had first introduced me to the brothers. She rushed over, her face aged with worry. 'Sal, what on earth happened? The news. I got back last night. What happened?'

There was a low wall at the edge of the car park, part of a bank edged with shrubs. We perched among the fragrance of lavender and dog rose, surrounded by the murmur of bees while I gave her my account of the story.

'So it wasn't a protest,' she said. 'Some people are claiming it was a protest against his asylum refusal.'

'He was in no fit state, Rachel. He was panicking, as though he couldn't bear to be in his own skin any longer. He was distraught. I'm so sorry.' I had to close my eyes – they were stinging – and blow my nose. 'Ramin,' I carried on, 'he doesn't want to see me. Is there anything you can do to help him?'

'I'll see,' she said. She laid a hand on my arm and the warmth steadied me. 'That's why I'm here.'

Ray was home by midday. The police had called to tell me I could collect my car and he was driving me there.

'You ready then?'

I must have looked scared or upset because he understood straightaway. 'Oh, Sal.'

'I don't want to go.' My throat was tight, my voice squeaky. He hugged me. The contact took the edge off my apprehension.

'I can't drive two,' he said. 'Do you want me to take someone else? Diane?'

'No. It's all right. Let's go.'

As we drove closer to the services, my dread returned. Feeling my muscles stiffen and my palms sweat, I took deliberate slow breaths in through my nose and out through my mouth. Ray took the slip road and prickles bloomed along my spine, buzzing filled my head and my guts twisted. Outwardly, I probably seemed fine. The disassociation between inward turmoil and outward calm is something I'm practised at. At times like that, there's a sort of muffled quality to my interaction with people and the real world while inside my nerves are singing and my imagination roars in morbid, savage overdrive.

The place looked completely normal, unruffled. Hard to credit that Berfan had died here barely forty-eight hours ago. Pictures of him danced round the back of my brain. I wouldn't look at them. I stared out of the window. My car was exactly where it had been. I gripped the spare keys in my hand.

'You OK?' Ray said as he parked.

'I need petrol,' I blurted out, 'I just can't—'

'Give me your keys.'

A few minutes later, he was back. 'That's done. You all right?'

'Fine,' I lied.

He caught the brittle note. 'Sal?'

'For now, I'm fine.' Fighting to control my voice. 'I just want to get home.'

'OK.'

'Don't follow me or anything,' I snapped. 'I can't bear that convoy stuff.'

He fought a smile. 'OK.'

'And don't laugh at me.' I knew what I was doing, as I said it, like a dog barking to make it feel brave.

Ray dipped his head.

He'd driven off by the time I was in my car. I put my seat belt on. I started the engine and drove slowly round to the filling station and pulled up by the air machine. Turning off the engine, I sat for a few minutes, summoning the courage to look at the spot where Berfan had fallen. I forced my eyes across, stared. There was nothing. No tell-tale marks on the ground, no chalk outline or dark stain, no cards or bunches of flowers.

Closing my eyes, I said a godless prayer for him. In the glove compartment I had a copy of the photograph Ramin had given me: the two brothers in their football kit with their friend. *Berfan is the top scorer.* What would have saved him? What would have helped? My throat ached but I didn't shed any tears. And then I drove home on auto-pilot.

As the shock eased, I experienced see-sawing emotions. I'd get angry in a great whoosh of intensity and tearful or anxious just as suddenly. It was difficult going to busy places; the shops or school, because I'd see Berfan out of the corner of my eye, disappearing into the crowd. The mind plays those tricks, I knew that, but even so my body fell for it every time. Sweat pricked at my armpits and the skin on my back shrank, my heart broke into a gallop and my mouth went dry.

When someone down the road had a barbecue, and the oily, meaty smell drifted over our garden, I found myself vomiting in the toilet, closing the windows and curling up in my bed.

Tranquilisers and anti-depressants helped. Counselling helped more. And walking. I walked miles. Upon the pavements of the city, their surface a mish-mash of different coloured tarmac, bands of it snaking along, sections laid this way and that. Testament to all the holes that had been dug for cables to be laid and pipes repaired. Now and then, I'd come across a fresh stretch of pavement, usually by some new-built flats, glistening clean and black and unbroken in contrast to the rest. I walked through streets embraced by forest trees, the leaves sprinkling the ground, roots cracking the kerbstones. Through green tunnels with stars of golden light piercing the canopy and catching seeds and flies in narrow beams. Past gardens and hedges and fences, doorways and windows each rich with clues as to the taste and wealth and quirks of the people inside.

I wandered through parks, past lakes peppered with ducks and gulls and geese, where crisp packets and sweet wrappers rimmed the shores like urban jetsam. I followed the river from Fletcher's Moss, where the botanical gardens are, along the top bank past Simon's Bridge, and around the curves to Northenden. Beyond the motorway flyover, I stopped at the weir, by the salmon race, and watched the water spill like boiling mercury, mesmerised by the repeating patterns in the cascade. I trekked along the river's lazy meanders past golf courses and pylons, with the ever-present roar of the motorway in my ears. Catching sight of a cormorant diving into the water. And a kingfisher flashing past, a daub of turquoise brilliantine, like magic.

I walk past mansions and maisonettes, flats and terraced rows. The older ones raised over a hundred and fifty years ago as the city boomed and the people poured in from the countryside to sell their labour, or hire it, in the industrial revolution.

I walk past the cemetery where they lie, where Berfan's ashes are, where Janet will be laid to rest, but I do not go in.

I walk.

I walk away my sadness and my fear. My limbs loosen, my feet ache, my heart relaxes. I catch some colour from the sun.

And I walk myself home.

CHAPTER TWENTY-SIX

The phone rang early. It was Trisha Marlowe. 'Looks like you were wrong,' she said.

'Sorry?'

'Mark's alibi. They've arrested him again. Steve says they'll probably charge him this time. They've obviously not found anyone else. You are still working for him?'

Was I? It was hard to concentrate. I'd been so wrapped up in the aftermath of Berfan's death that everything else seemed distant and muddled. 'Trisha, can I ring you back sometime? Things have been a bit chaotic here, another case.'

'Oh.' She was taken aback. 'Yes, sorry. Yes, that's fine. Just thought you'd want to know.'

Janet Florin. I thought of the quarry. Trisha's fears, *I keep thinking of her, really scared and knowing that she's going to die. Do you think she knew?* Who was with her that day? It was only a few miles from the garage in Grassington to the quarry. The police would have interviewed possible witnesses. Had they taken Mark into custody again because someone had been seen with her who looked like Mark? Or had they got some forensic evidence? Had I been wrong, again, about him?

Digger padded into the room and whined at me.

'What?'

He whined again. Eyes beseeching, his pointed nose surrounded by greying hairs.

'I never take you for a walk if I'm not running.'

His tail plunged up and down.

'OK – but don't make a habit of it.'

There were already a scattering of people in the park: serious joggers and other people taking their dogs for a morning constitutional. I limbered up a bit then ran with Digger at my heels. Lack of sleep sapped my energy, so I didn't push myself. The grass was drenched with dew and under the trees spiders' webs lanced with light were hung with golden beads. Squirrels and blackbirds foraged and a heron flew across the park like some Jurassic beast, huge wings beating slowly, sharp beak pointing the way. The first conker cases sprouted on the horse chestnut trees, tiny spiky orbs like maces in lime green.

When I'd slowed to a walk, Digger exchanged sniffs with some of the other dogs. A couple of owners recognised Digger and greeted him by name. I felt like an interloper in their doggy world. He barked at a flock of pigeons that were loitering hopefully by the duck pond, most of them ignored him.

By the time we got home, the household was stirring and I had come to a decision. I'd found Berfan only to see him die. I couldn't do anything for Ramin. Janet Florin was dead, too. Last seen buying soft toys at a garage. Found floating in a quarry. Hit then pushed. I couldn't help Janet but I now believed Mark Florin was an innocent man. There must be more I could do to help him fight his corner.

You are still working for him? Trisha had asked me.

Yes, I thought, if he'll have me, if they'll pay me, I'll carry on. Both Lily Shen and Trisha believed that Janet had never articulated her misgivings about Oliver Tennant, the teacher she suspected of fraud. But, according to Mrs Tennant, Janet did say something. So when? If Janet had made the allegations just before her death then perhaps Oliver had taken desperate measures. In that case, his wife had no idea what he had done or she'd never have shot her mouth off to me about the whole business.

A phone call with Piers Carruthers confirmed that Mark had been rearrested.

'Have they new evidence?'

'Not exactly. The police couldn't find the girls in Liverpool but the barman admits to seeing him there, though he insists he can't be sure which day it was. What he did say was that it was lunchtime and Mark didn't stay long.'

'So he'd have time to drive to Yorkshire.'

'Unfortunately. A couple of hours would cover it, apparently.'

'I was thinking of retracing Janet's steps, if you want me to carry on, see if there's anything more to be gained from talking to people up there.'

'Excellent,' he said.

So, apparently, I was still on board. 'There's also some bad feeling with a previous colleague that I want to find out more about.' I gave him the gist of the Oliver Tennant story, though he was less interested in this, sticking to his position of concentrating on defending Mark rather than finding other suspects.

'I need to speak to Mark again,' I said.

'Leave it with me.'

A lawyer is entitled to visit his client and with some persistence Carruthers was able to get that privilege extended to me. He rang me back with the arrangement. A police officer would be monitoring the conversation.

Mark Florin looked worse than ever and smelt bad too. That same rank scent of fear. There was a weariness to him, a defeat that had replaced his rage. Could he remember any time in the last year when Janet had been away overnight?

'Just the once. She had a residential training weekend. Health and safety, I think.'

'When?'

'I'm not sure. January, February. Why?'

'She may not have been on a course,' I explained.

Silence. He looked at me stonily and then his face seemed to collapse a little as he lowered his eyes.

'I'm sorry.'

'Who?' he said, as he folded one large hand in the other.

'I don't know. I'm trying to find out.'

It was a tiny step forward but how to make progress? I needed to track down the hotel. Buxton's a popular spa town, the jewel of the peaks. There are loads of hotels there.

I rooted out my copies of the Florins' financial documents and looked back through to the spring credit card statements. It was there in black and white. *Peak View Hotel £37.50.* An odd amount. I searched online and found the hotel website. Among the treats available to guests was a session in the spa and beauty suite for £37.50. Presumably, her lover had paid for the weekend. At that point, her card was £7,967 in the red. An extra £37.50 must have felt irrelevant. And if Mark ever looked at the statement, she could tell him it was some cost incurred during the training course. For me, there was the fillip of finding another piece of the story but I was no nearer finding out the man's name.

Even if I could bribe someone to let me peruse the registers from Peak View Hotel, how would I ever know which name and address represented the man Janet had spent the weekend with?

Faced with a dead end on that line of inquiry, I got myself organised to visit the quarry where Janet had died.

Ray looked at me askance when I told him. 'Don't you think you ought to take it easy?'

'I can't just sit around and mope.'

'It's hardly moping.'

'Ray, I think I know what I can handle.'

He gave a derisory snort.

'What's that supposed to mean?'

Followed by a theatrical sigh.

Oh God, I thought, he's going to sulk on me. Most of our sticky moments in the past have been related to my work, times when he thought I was being reckless – either that or arguments about housework. Anyway, this time he pulled himself back from the icy steppes of withdrawal and answered. 'You've had a horrendous experience. Don't you need some time to recover?'

'Yes, but it's not like I can take three weeks out and it'll all be hunky-dory. I'm already seeing the counsellor. I want to keep busy.'

'You make it sound like you're going to sort the cupboards out or do the ironing. This woman's been killed.' He was getting agitated now.

'But I think he's innocent. I don't like the guy much but things don't add up. All I'm doing is going over what we know of the woman's movements and trying to come up with a plausible story.'

'You're trying to find the killer.'

Silence.

'You want me to pick the kids up?' he asked, a cool edge to his voice.

'Yes. I've no idea when I'll be back.' Being churlish myself now. I made to leave then regretted my pettiness and turned to him. 'I should be back for tea.'

He stood with his arms crossed. 'Hope so,' he said. 'It's your turn to cook.'

I nearly fell for it. 'For God's sake, Ray…' Then I caught the gleam in his eyes. I moved close. Thumped his shoulder.

'You, you—'

He stopped me speaking, pulled me close and kissed me hard. I kissed him harder.

'Don't be late,' he said, letting me go.

'Don't tell me what to do,' I said as I walked away.

CHAPTER TWENTY-SEVEN

In stark contrast to my previous journey up to the Dales, the weather was grey and misty, the sky blank and bleak. Now and again I had to use the wipers to clear the fine moisture from the windows. But even a lowering sky couldn't detract from the luminous green of the pastures and the light limestone walls.

My thoughts led repeatedly to Berfan and Ramin and I felt the weight of sadness between my shoulder blades. Something I had to carry with me. As I passed the small garage in Grassington where Janet had bought toys for her children, I felt an eddy of anxiety. What was I doing there? Making a last-ditch attempt to unpick the mystery? Proving to myself that I could still function? Trying to do better for Mark Florin than I had for Ramin?

From Grassington, I took the road that led up one of the smaller dales to higher ground. The road bucked and turned, offering glimpses of farmsteads and tumbling streams, the smooth hillsides laced with walls. Mist became cloud and I slowed to a crawl. If this was the route Janet took, then there was nowhere to stop for lunch: no inns with home-cooked food or hotels with en suite rooms. Reaching the summit in second gear, it was a couple of miles to the quarry, the far side of a hamlet called Tarnghyll. Presumably it had housed the quarrymen and their families. It nestled in a shallow bowl-shaped depression, a triangular village green at the centre bounded by rows of cottages on three sides. The buildings huddled against the ground with small doors and windows, protection from the bitter winters they'd get up here. Most of them had tubs and mangers planted with pansies, ivy, geranium and fuchsia. There was a small Norman church, with a square tower, at the apex of the green and a more modern building peeped out behind it with a sloping roof. One of the cottages nearby had been a local shop and post office but was now boarded up and for sale. The place was quiet. I couldn't see a soul.

Driving out of the top of the hamlet, past the church and the hall at the back, it took just a few minutes to reach the quarry. There was a lay-by of sorts and a weathered board which warned *Danger: Deep Water*. No fencing. I walked across the grass, the ten or twelve yards to the edge where white stones were laid out at intervals.

From that vantage point the hillside fell away, gradually at first before plunging down to the water a hundred feet below. The still surface of the lake was a creamy brown colour, like caramel ice cream. If Janet had fallen here, she wouldn't have landed in the lake. Further round though the drop was sheer, a cliff face of hewn limestone dotted with straggling gorse bushes, clumps of bracken and patches of heather. Making my way along the perimeter, as the banks became steeper, I trod carefully, anxious not to trip. A rush of vertigo, the sudden sickening fear that I might lose control and hurl myself over the precipice, persuaded me to sit down. Spreading my waterproof on the grass, I could feel the tussocks springy beneath.

There were birds crying across the other side and the quarry seemed to amplify their calls. Peewits, I thought, moorland birds with a lonely, piping cry.

Had they come here for a picnic? Janet and her killer? Or to walk? Had they spent a long leisurely afternoon somewhere else and then come up here? But she'd intended to pick up her kids.

So he'd brought her here and then what? A quarrel, a fight about something getting more heated, more vicious until he hit her? Picked up a stone, there were plenty scattered in the grass, and hit her. Or flung her against one. Then, knowing or not knowing she lived, he'd pushed her down, over the edge, watching until she sank in the water. And then he'd driven off.

I gazed for long enough at the crater and the brown opaque lagoon below, at the birds looping above and the flash of a rabbit's tail on the slope. Running my hands over the tufted grass, I made out tiny bells on a sprig of pink heather, the exotic shape of a birdsfoot trefoils, which reminded me of sweet peas or wisteria. I saw spiders with pea-sized bodies and long, long, thin legs and everywhere the spiky cotton grass was shivering in the faintest breeze. The mist was light here but the vapour brought out the pungent note in the smells of grass and bracken.

Once upon a time, the quarry would have been chaotic with men and horse-drawn wagons, thick with lime dust and rubble. Blasting the rock from the hills. Busy with stonecutters and masons who were supplying the burgeoning city palaces of the industrial revolution. Providing limestone columns for town halls and corn exchanges. Limestone floors and steps, porticos and curlicues for banks and assurance companies, hotels and arcades. Gruelling work for the quarrymen and the masons who were at risk of having their limbs crushed by falling stone and who would live and die with the white dust in their lungs.

A violent place in the past and now again a place of sudden violent death.

My sandwiches and coffee were in the car. I thought I'd have them by the village green. If the shop had still been open I could have called in and tried to pick up any gossip about the police inquiry, whether any local witnesses had come forward. Re-entering the hamlet from the other side, I saw a sign I'd missed earlier for parking, toilets and play area by the church hall. As good as place as any. And with a two-hour journey home ahead of me, it made sense to use the facilities.

The car park was empty. It was modest, room for perhaps a dozen vehicles. A noticeboard in wood and etched steel announced that Tarnghyll's community hall and playground had been built with help from the Millennium Fund. I walked round the building. It was hexagonal with limestone walls and a steeply pitched roof giving it the flavour of a tee-pee or a circus tent. Not old-fashioned though for it had solar panels on the far side, facing south. The place reminded me of something. Probably something in Manchester where weird and wonderful buildings were going up all the time. The solar panels wouldn't generate anything much on day as dull as this. Wouldn't a windmill have been a better choice? The back of the building had a run of glass doors and a semi-circular terrace looking out onto a delightful playground. Maddie and

Tom would have loved it. Wooden roundabouts and climbing frames but also some unusual rides: a large wooden rocking horse that could seat six, a wobbly wooden crocodile, a swing boat. Picnic tables around the place were carved in the shape of wildlife: rabbit and hedgehog, owl and stoat (or weasel – I can't tell the difference).

The toilets off to the side were clean and freshly painted. That's always a welcome surprise. I ate my sandwiches at the hedgehog table, sipped at my coffee.

There was a gate into the churchyard, so afterwards I thought I'd have a look around before starting my journey home. I went through and wandered about. There were some very old graves in one corner, the stones lay flat in the turf. Stories of Thomas Cook of Ripon and his wife Elizabeth with three children dead in infancy, or Mary Thwaite of Settle who had married Edward Preston and died in childbirth, her daughter Martha had survived until the age of eight, and then there was Jacob Langley who had lived until the grand old age of seventy. His three score years and ten.

There weren't many new graves; perhaps the graveyard was full. The ones from the 1970s, small upright stones in speckled marble, looked flimsy besides the dark weathered slabs of their ancestors.

'Brightening up.' The woman smiled at me. Middle-aged, angular, lank hair and nice teeth, she wore corduroy pants, a jerkin, and a dog collar (the religious type not the S&M variety). She carried a trug, a trowel and some shears.

'Yes, it is.'

'Walking?'

'Working.'

Her look became a little more guarded. 'Are you a journalist?'

I must have looked puzzled. She nodded at my shoes. 'You've been out at the quarry.' They were covered in white dust. Couldn't the police establish whether Mark Florin's car had been out there? Whether there was quarry dust in the tread of his tyres, or on his shoes? Was that why they'd arrested him again?

'No,' I replied. 'I'm a private detective assisting the defence for Mark Florin.'

'Very sad business.'

'Yes. No one here saw anything.' I said it as a statement rather than a fact, seeing if she'd put me right.

'No. Most of the villagers commute to work. The police have arrested him, haven't they?'

'Yes.'

'We had a murder here, once before,' she told me. '1780.' As though it had been yesterday. 'There was a young woman who worked in the quarry. One of the maids who helped with the carts. She fell in love with the quarry-owner's son, he told her she was his sweetheart and one day they would marry. She fell pregnant. Her family approached the owner to make arrangements and he sent for his son. The son denied everything. He claimed the girl was bewitched and had lain with Satan. The following morning the girl was found floating in the quarry, stones in her pockets. She had drowned herself. The son went missing. They searched for him all over. Nothing. They found him the following spring, down one of the deep gorges in the quarry workings, his neck broken. Some claimed the girl had spirited him there, others that her father had taken revenge. Nothing was ever proven but it is said that their ghosts haunt the quarry: he calls for help in the dark, she cries for justice.'

'I didn't think the Church went in for superstition.'

'No, but justice is pretty high up on the agenda.' She smiled again. 'And it's a great story.'

I could imagine the villagers were already telling Janet's tale to each other. Once her killer was known, it would have a neat punchline. Would she be allocated a ghost? Another thought struck me. What if Janet's killer was a local man? Someone she maybe met in Manchester but who said he wanted to show her his home turf? He'd know about the quarry, off the beaten track as far as tourists were concerned, and the legends I'd just heard.

'Does anybody here work in Manchester, have connections there?'

'Yes, Ralph Carrington. He doesn't commute every day. They're still trying to sell their place in Manchester, so he's there during the week and the family are up here.'

My heart stumbled. Was he the one? The one she'd spent Monday nights with? The one she'd checked into a Buxton hotel with? The one she'd come up here with on that last fateful day? I fought to concentrate on what the vicar was saying. 'They had an offer but the buyers pulled out at the last minute.'

My mind was scurrying back and forth with questions and suppositions. He'd have been taking a helluva risk coming up here with Janet. In a place so small, people would recognise his car. Though that could work to his advantage perhaps, because it would go unremarked. It would blend in unlike a stranger's vehicle. And he'd have a pretty good idea of who was likely to be home, who'd be safely out of the way on a weekday. I hadn't seen a soul, except the vicar.

'What does he do?'

'He teaches.'

My scalp tightened. 'Where?'

'MMU.'

Manchester Metropolitan University. Not a school then.

'Some of his students did placements helping on our Millennium Hall,' she said.

'And Mrs Carrington?'

The vicar raised her head slightly, tilted it back and studied me. I think my nosiness was beginning to concern her. Nevertheless, she answered. 'She's with the bank in Settle.'

So she'd be out at work, away from the village, during the week. I could sense the vicar was going to start quizzing me, so I mumbled something about trying to find out how Janet knew the place and left it at that. She seemed to accept it.

'Well, I must get on.' She nodded at the graves. 'Jill of all trades.'

I felt light-headed on the way back. A gassy sensation of excitement in my nervous system. Maybe I'd found Janet's lover. Yes, it was all supposition but he had connections to the city and to the quarry, he was away from his wife on Monday nights. At the very least, he bore more scrutiny. Had Janet ever worked at MMU? As far as I knew, there were pretty strict divisions between the different areas of education: teachers tended to train and teach in primary, secondary, further or higher education. There were probably links between high schools and the local universities, so staff in the same subject areas might well know each other. But Janet had taught at primary school. The other end of the spectrum.

Back in my office, I logged on and went into the MMU website. Ralph Carrington taught in the Department of Environmental and Geographical Science. His email and phone number were listed. When I cross-referenced it to the Florins' phone bill there was no match. But she could have rung his mobile, or his home number, used her own mobile. Was I grasping at straws? Surely the police would have interviewed all local residents in Tarnghyll. If Ralph Carrington had said he was in Manchester all week, would they have bothered to corroborate it? If I could find out his timetable at the university and engineer a way to check out whether he'd given lectures or tutorials on June 10th it would be easy to eliminate him. If he'd not been in the university then, it might be worth mentioning it to DC Whittaker. Though I didn't relish the prospect of another bout with her.

My phone rang. It was Lily Shen, Janet's teaching assistant, again.

'I've talked to the police about Oliver Tennant,' she said. 'They didn't seem very interested. I felt like I was wasting their time.'

'Well, it's better to have told them,' I said, 'even if they discount it. Do you know whether they'll see Mr Tennant?'

'No. And then I started thinking what if Janet had it all wrong? I'd hate to be responsible for the bloke losing his job.' Lily sighed.

'There's not much chance of that if he's honest.'

'Hope you're right.'

After the call, I thought some more about Oliver Tennant. If Janet had confronted him very close to her disappearance, then what was the catalyst for her taking action? Why did she suddenly want to put things right? It was frustrating second-guessing with so little to go on. And she'd not breathed a word to anyone. Kept it secret from the world. Even from her best friend, Trisha. Like she had with the affair. Are friends allowed secrets? Diane and I didn't hide anything from each other. Not that I knew of. I'd told her about Ray – well, not initially when that first unsettling moment of physical attraction had taken us both by surprise. Partly because I'd still been fathoming it out. But I'd shared everything, including that, since. Diane had confided in me in the past, even when she became entangled in relationships that I thought were bad for her. We'd argued about things like that but it hadn't led to either of us keeping secrets. Our relationship was strong enough to bear the weight of different opinions.

Perhaps for Trisha and Janet there had been an imbalance in the friendship. Had Trisha invested it with more importance, more intimacy than Janet? Trisha baring her soul but Janet selecting which parts of her life she wanted to share.

Never having met Janet, I had only a partial grasp of her personality but if I was asked, I'd have selected Trisha as the more powerful one. She was wealthy and confident and her marriage wasn't plagued by the unhappiness of Janet's. Had Janet ever suspected that Mark visited prostitutes? Was that something else she had learnt and kept from Trisha?

Something that made it more likely she'd look for affection outside the marriage. Perhaps Janet feared if she confided in Trisha she would be shown pity, or given advice she didn't want. What makes people decide to share or conceal? Trust, fear, the need for privacy? It must have been hard for Janet to carry those secrets; it would be for me, to have no outlet, nobody to pick over them with. But I wasn't Janet Florin. Perhaps she got a thrill from it. They say illicit sex is often spicier. Did her secret life, her mystery man, help make her miserable marriage and her tough teaching jobs tolerable?

Carrington and Tennant. Two men who might be connected to the murder. I decided not to contact DC Whittaker yet, not until I'd progressed further with gathering information on Carrington. And if that left me none the wiser, then I'd tell the police that Mrs Tennant could identify Janet's secret lover. And possibly her killer.

CHAPTER TWENTY-EIGHT

Diane's appointment for her lumpectomy was for the following day. She was complaining at having to fast beforehand. 'I know why,' she grumbled. 'But surely if I stopped eating at five it'd all be processed by tomorrow morning. I'm starving already.'

'I'll bring you something in, for when you come round. What do you fancy?'

Her eyes gleamed. 'Hot and sour Thai seafood soup, noodles, stir fried rice and beef teriyaki.'

My face fell at the scope of her request.

'Sal, you don't have to kill it or cook it,' she referred to my veggie sensibilities, 'just bring it. And some of that carrot cake from the deli.'

'Deal.'

'You sure you're OK?'

I'd told her as little as I could get away with about Berfan. She'd enough to deal with.

'Yeah. Pissed off and sad, really.'

She nodded. 'And Ray?'

I smiled. She fluttered her eyebrows then fell serious. She made a play of fiddling with her hair. 'Be careful, won't you.'

'He always uses a condom.'

'Not that. Don't get hurt.'

'You were the one who—'

'I know. But if anything goes wrong, it's not just him, is it? It's the kids, the house.'

Astounding. Diane, my reckless friend, was sounding like me at my most cautious.

'That's exactly what I said to you in the first place. It's a bit late now. And it's good.'

'Whooo!'

'I don't know where it's going or any of that but I don't want to worry about it while it's still good.'

'Message received. God,' she screwed up her face, 'I could kill for a chocolate biscuit.'

I rang MMU and got put through to the secretary in the Department of Environmental and Geographical Science. 'I'm ringing to see about Mr Carrington's availability,' I told her. 'We run a local discussion group, we invite people in to talk to us about aspects of their work. I wonder if Mr Carrington might be able to come along? We meet every Thursday.'

'Well, you're probably best writing to him,' she said. 'Term's nearly over anyway and we don't have the timetable through for next semester.'

'Does he usually teach on Thursdays?'

'It doesn't work like that. He's not had lectures on Thursdays this year but it can change completely from one academic year to the next.'

So he was free on Thursdays. I thanked the woman and rang off.

I couldn't rule Carrington out but could I find any further

connection between him and Janet? Using the Internet I came up with an address and then eventually a home phone number for him. But it didn't appear on the Florins' phone records.

Back to basics, I told myself. It made sense to go back to the beginning, to work through my notes and see whether anything jumped out at me.

Settling with coffee, I used Blu-Tack to fix a sheet of A1 paper to the wall. At the top, I wrote Janet's name. Anything that appeared significant went up there under subheadings: Mark/Marriage, Mystery Lover and Other.

When I'd finished I had three lists:

Mark/Marriage
  Debts/job insecurity/life insurance policy
  Mark using prostitutes
  Lied initially
  Janet devoted to kids

Mystery Lover
  Prob killer – went to Yorkshire
  Knew quarry
  Monday nights
  Ralph Carrington?
  Life of leisure/cancelled hair/ new clothes – planning to leave Mark

Other
  Oliver Tennant – a lot to lose – motive
  Knew about J's lover – blackmail

Then I reviewed my timeline for Janet's last proven movements. Janet had seemed fine to Mark on that Thursday morning. And to Trisha who had spoken with her the previous evening. She hadn't said anything about tackling Oliver Tennant. She'd given the impression that the next day would be a mundane one, pottering and doing housework. I picked up the phone records. There had been two calls to the Marlowes', one at 8.05 p.m. and a second at 11.30 p.m. The first lasted four minutes, the second just five. Had Trisha been able to remember any more of the content of those conversations? She was settling Isobel when I rang. Steve offered to pass on a message. 'I'd like to come out and talk to her, first thing in the morning if that suits?'

'She takes the children into school, she's trying to keep some routine going for them... She's generally back here about 9.30.'

'Fine, I'll call then. Perhaps she could ring me back soon, if that's not convenient.'

She did ring back. She needed to shop the following morning and was meeting a friend for lunch.

'Have you time now?' I could have talked over the phone but communication is so much better face to face.

She hesitated. Her attitude to me had undergone a sea change since I'd agreed to work for Mark. I understood her point of view; she believed he might have killed the friend she loved. Her reply was cool, but polite as she always was. 'If you wish.'

It was the end of the day as I pulled into the Marlowes' drive. A wind had got up, clearing the cloud and now there was a hint of pink against the silhouette of the hills, promising fair weather for the following day.

Hector, the red setter, bounded out, sniffing at me. Steve invited me in. Trisha looked striking in a white cotton shift that set off the warm brown of her skin. A gold chain at her neck was her only decoration. She nodded at me but didn't smile.

'You don't need me?' Steve looked from Trisha to me.

'No,' I said.

'I'll, erm...' he pointed across the large room to the work area in the corner.

'He never stops,' Trisha said fondly. Her manner thawed. She was simply too nice to maintain a frosty façade for long.

'How are the kids?' I asked her as we sat.

'It's really hard. There's a big difference between playing godmother and having them 24/7. Jacob's a handful. If they charge Mark... I don't know what we'll do. Steve, he's not very good with them—' She broke off frowning. 'When you're asked to be godmother you don't ever think about a situation like this.'

'It's a lot to take on,' I acknowledged. 'It might not come to that. I think Mark's telling the truth. I think Janet was seeing someone, and planning to leave the marriage, perhaps move in with him. Either that or—' I was going to tell her about Oliver Tennant but she interrupted.

'But the children?'

'I know. Maybe she intended taking the children.'

'She'd have said.'

My phone sounded. I apologised as I pulled it out. A text message from Ray. *X*. A single kiss. My cheeks glowed. I put my phone down.

'The Monday nights – she'd been going to that yoga class for a few years?'

'Yes. We went together way back in the beginning but my mum's in a home now and I go over there on Mondays, spend the evening with her.'

'Was there anyone at the night class that showed a special interest in Janet?'

'No.'

'She ever mention someone nice there?'

'I've told you, no. I've racked my brains. She never mentioned another man to me.'

'Have you ever heard the name Ralph Carrington?'

'No. Who is he?'

'Someone she may have run into, but I don't know yet. That Wednesday evening when she called you about eightish, what did you talk about? Please try and remember the details.'

'Erm, Mark's interview,' she said acidly. 'How she hoped he'd get it and how glad she was that she'd finished work, be nice to potter about. That was it.'

'And when she rang later?'

Trisha frowned.

'There was another call at half past eleven.'

'No. I'd have been in bed anyway. Unless she spoke to Steve.'

Realisation slammed into my chest like a fist and panic followed. Janet had called the Marlowes' late on the Wednesday night, and spoken for five minutes. She'd been skipping yoga every Monday for months – the same day her best friend Trisha was tied up visiting her aged mother. Leaving the coast clear.

All along, Trisha had protested: I'd have known if she were seeing anyone, she'd have told me. Oh no, she wouldn't, I thought, you'd be the last person she'd tell.

'Steve,' Trisha called. He stood up. 'Did you take a call from Janet late on the Wednesday night?'

'Yes,' he said. 'She wanted to ask you about babysitting, they'd had some invite. You were asleep. Is it important?' He looked worried, sounded anxious to help.

'No,' I smiled, felt as though my lips would shatter. I turned back to Trisha. 'I'll be getting off now. Thanks.'

She was a little disconcerted by the abrupt end to our meeting. I could feel Steve's eyes boring into my back as I walked out. Had he heard me state where my thoughts led about Janet and her lover? Did he know what I suspected?

I said goodbye to Trisha at the door then crunched my way across the gravel, my thoughts scuttling like creatures in panic. Hurriedly, I opened my car door and slid into my seat. A flash of movement reflected in the rearview mirror. Steve! Coming out, coming after me. My fingers gripped the ignition key hard, I twisted it and gunned the engine, heard it stall. He was running, his face contorted, shouting. Shit! Please, I prayed to the car, turning the key again and again, my foot pumping the accelerator. The engine caught as he reached me, he banged on the rear windscreen, I jolted at the noise and floored the accelerator, the car screaming away in a clattering spray of gravel.

Twilight smothered the hillsides as I hared down, away from their home. The moon, fat and creamy, shone through mist which blurred its edges. In my rearview mirror I could see the yellow light gleaming from their stunning stretch of windows, saw the solar panels glinting in the moonlight. Solar panels. The community hall in Yorkshire had reminded me of something. Now I knew why. It was similar in style to the Marlowes' house. And if Steve Marlowe's firm had a hand in the design then he'd know about the quarry.

I fought to follow the twisting, narrow road, my hands clamped to the steering wheel, my wrists aching. There were no streetlights in that section. Headlights glared behind me. Oh, God, he was chasing me! Fright nettled my forearms. He'd killed her and I had worked it out and he knew. We were on our own; there were no other houses along the lane. He was coming to get me. To shut me up.

I gathered speed, eager to gain the main road. As I crested a rise, I could see the line of orange streetlights marking the route along the valley bottom. I'd be safer there. I didn't know the area well enough to try and throw him off my trail so my only hope was to get home and once there to call the police.

The road plunged down a steep slope to the T-junction at the bottom. A large shape darted across my headlights. A badger! I slammed my foot on the brake; the seatbelt bit into my breastbone. Any other time, I'd have loved to see a wild badger but now it meant Steve Marlowe had caught up to me. He flashed his lights. As if I'd pull over and stop for him.

Accelerating hard, I skidded onto the main road and broke the speed limit on the stretch towards Manchester, leaving it till the last minute to veer off onto the M60 link that would take me in the direction of home. I was panting, talking aloud, partly to reassure myself but also to give vent to some of the fury I felt for the man. A mix of pep talk and curses.

I thought I'd lost him. I willed my pulse to slow, my heartbeat to settle. It's all right, I reassured myself, nearly there, it's all right. Then he reappeared and my heart hammered hard and fast. At the roundabout by the Co-op pyramid building he was still a few cars behind me. Ray will be there, I told myself, just get home. I kept a lead all the way along Didsbury Road, jumping a red light at one point and swerving round parked cars near the parade of shops. There was a queue at the junction with Kingsway and I watched in the mirror as a number of cars drew up in my wake. But not Steve's. Had he given up, turned back? I gave a shaky sigh of relief then the ominous silhouette of his 4x4 reared up on the horizon. Terror knifed at my heart and I swore again.

When the lights changed to green, I drove as quickly as I could, overtaking the stream of cars and then shifting from the right-hand lane to the nearside at the Parrswood crossroads. A driver sounded his horn in protest.

Against all the odds the traffic was light along Didsbury high street. Some of the cars between us turned off until there were only two vehicles separating us. As I neared home, my anxiety didn't lessen any. He was so close. I couldn't catch my breath. My chest was heavy with pressure. I didn't signal or slow as we came along Wilmslow Road into Withington. In fact I sped up and turned into my street at the last minute with a howl of brakes as the car swung from side to side and a crunch as it clipped the wing mirror of a parked camper van. Marlowe sailed past.

I pulled into our drive and slammed on the brakes, leapt out, fumbling for my house keys. I dropped them, crouched to snatch them back and ran to the door, pushing the Yale key in with trembling fingers.

Ray came into the hall and his smile faded to consternation when he saw the state I was in.

I heard an engine outside, the slam of a car door.

'He's after me,' I hissed at Ray.

His face darkened. 'Who?'

Knocking at the door.

Ray, who was angry rather than fearful, moved to open it. 'Ray!' I tried to warn him not to but it was too late. He swung it back. Steve Marlowe stood there. He nodded at Ray then looked at me. 'You left your phone,' he said, holding it out towards me. 'You always drive like that?'

My pulse was pounding, blood thundering in my neck. I stepped forward and took my phone, trying to force a normal expression into my face. 'Thanks.'

Ray looked edgy, unsure what he was expected to do.

There was an awkward pause and then Steve Marlowe said. 'See you, then.' There was no threat in his tone. He turned and walked away. I heard him get into his car and drive off.

Ray looked at me, waiting for an explanation.

'I need to check something,' I told him. I went through and turned on the computer. Ray hovered in the background as I typed in Steve Marlowe and got thousands of hits. Flipping through my notes, I found the details from my first trip. I typed again: *renewable energy, consultants, Marlowe.* I clicked on the first link, my tongue pressed hard against the roof of my mouth as I waited for the page to load.

There it was. On the home page, a shot of the conical church hall in Tarnghyll. The wall of glass was visible, the solar panels. Features that had felt familiar because they were so similar to those on the Marlowes' house.

Why kill her? Why? Couldn't he have just walked away?

What did he have to gain from her death? Freedom? Keeping his own marriage intact?

Had the killing been planned? Perhaps. The location was convenient: an isolated spot with an abandoned quarry to dump the corpse. Hadn't he realised that the body might float to the surface?

Perhaps it wasn't a plan. Just a violent mess. A debacle. And her disposal made in the flaring heat of panic.

But since then, Steve Marlowe had been a cool customer. With his cheery disposition, his concern for Trisha. It was ironic, and macabre, that he'd been landed with Janet's children while the police held Mark. *Steve, he's not very good with them*, Trisha had confided.

I pulled out Whittaker's card and began to push the numbers. There was no vengeful deputy principal, no mystery man from MMU, no greedy husband pulling double bluffs. Just her best friend's bloke. Who'd come racing after me in his 4x4. If I'd been here alone, if he hadn't seen Ray, what would he have said then? What would he have done? Did he think I'd swallowed his lie about that late night phone call? He was hard to read, he was clever, but I'd put it together now.

I listened to the phone ring, my hand tight on the receiver, my eyes fixed on Ray's. For me, there was no flicker of triumph, no sense of achievement, I just felt hollow and saddened. A little dirtied by the truth.

Whittaker answered impatiently. It was late.

'It's Sal Kilkenny,' I told her. 'I know who killed Janet Florin.'

CHAPTER TWENTY-NINE

Steve Marlowe was arrested that night at Manchester Airport. He claimed he was off on a business trip.

In the early hours, I was dreaming: there was an animal in the road, injured. It was crying, a repetitive, piercing yelp which dissolved as I woke to the phone ringing out.

Trisha Marlowe was almost incoherent. 'The police, it's Steve, it's…they arrested Mark, they arrested him twice…now Steve. They don't know what they're doing. It's a mistake. How can they think that? What did you say to them?'

'Trisha—'

Before I could form an adequate reply she spoke again. 'You don't honestly believe he had anything to do with it?'

The silence stretched out. I took a breath, readied myself.

She put the phone down.

Later that day, the police released Mark Florin. When I called at their house, I found him in the back garden with Jacob and Isobel. Mark looked even worse than he had when we'd met at the police station. His skin was pallid, putty-like, his mouth clamped tight in between speaking, as though he was fighting off nausea and his forehead glistened with drops of sweat. Again I smelt his sharp, meaty body odour. Should I suggest a shower and change of clothes while I watched the children? He'd probably feel better for it but I didn't want to risk offending him.

He sat on the garden bench and Isobel settled on his lap. His hand was absent-mindedly patting her leg. The gesture reminded me of the motion of comfort Isobel had made to Trisha, stroking her face. Presumably Trisha had dropped the kids back with Mark and was now embroiled in a new nightmare of her own.

Jacob was kicking a ball through the shrubs in the border to the fence behind. His face was impassive and he made a point of ignoring me.

There was no way I wanted to talk to Mark with the children listening so I suggested a trip out to Chorlton Meadows.

'OK,' Mark said.

'No!' Jacob kicked the ball again hard and a branch of buddleia snapped off with the impact. I could see Mark's hand trembling and sense his fatigue.

'The water park then.' It was a place I often took Maddie and Tom. 'We can get an ice cream on the way and there's a playground for Isobel.' Stressing that I understood that Jacob was way too old for playgrounds.

'Ice cream,' Isobel crowed, wriggling down from her dad's lap. She hopped from foot to foot.

Jacob's back tensed.

'C'mon Jake,' Mark said briskly. 'Bring the ball.'

With ice lollies in hand, the two children clambered about the wooden play structures. The lake glimmered, a glossy teal colour, and a flock of Canada geese patrolled the shore on the lookout for visitors with bread.

Mark was staring away across the water when he spoke. 'If I hadn't hired you—' He shook his head, gave an angry snort. 'There was no bloody apology, you know. Nothing. Just *thank you for your time, Mr Florin. A family liaison officer will be available to you.* I knew there was someone!' He turned to me, his chin jutting out as if challenging me to say otherwise. 'I told you.'

'Yes. I'm sorry. It's a terrible thing.'

'I hope he rots in hell.'

'Daddy!' Isobel called from the slide. He turned and watched her descend. The sun glanced off the silver metal and the air above shimmied in the heat.

'She was leaving me,' he said flatly.

I wasn't sure if it was a question but I answered him anyway. 'Yes.'

There was a long pause. Jacob swung along the monkey bars. Isobel hunkered down and was pulling a bit of a stick through the bark chippings on the ground.

Mark didn't say another word about Janet. I wondered how he felt. Whether inwardly he was cursing her for her betrayal, for the lies and deceit, or whether his heart ached with the loss of her. Perhaps he felt both these things. Perhaps guilty too: she wasn't the only one who'd played false – he'd had his secret visits to prostitutes, after all.

Sure that he'd finished, I nodded at Jacob, now walking up the slide, his trainers squeaking on the surface. 'The kids,' I said, 'they have counsellors nowadays, to help them deal with it. It's important.'

Mark glared at me and I waited for some barbed remark

but then his eyes relaxed and he took a deep breath in. Gave a terse grunt.

And you could do with some help yourself, I thought.

'You'll have to see Mr Carruthers about your money,' Mark said as we walked up the hill away from the lake and towards the car park. 'I've had a letter from the bank. They've frozen our accounts.'

You poor bloody man. I remembered Trisha's assessment of him: the bloke with a chip on his shoulder who took his wife for granted even though she and the kids were his whole life. He'd still got the kids but who could tell whether he'd be able to demonstrate his love for them or whether the embattled, embittered part of his personality would simply take over, feeding off the terrible events he'd lived through.

'Thanks,' he said as we parted. Just the one word and an echoing nod and then he steered Jacob and Isobel towards his car.

Trisha Marlowe rang me again a few days later. 'I wondered, if you're not too busy, if you've any time…'

'Yes,' I told her.

'I've a meeting in town this morning,' she said. 'Legal stuff.'

'Steve?'

'They've charged him,' she said quietly. 'He's on remand in custody. So—' she went on quickly before I could respond, 'I should be free about one. I could come to you?'

'Or I can come into town if that's easier?'

We arranged to meet in the café in Urbis. The Museum of the City had taken a while to find favour in Manchester;

people admired the architecture – the milky-green glass with a pronounced wedge shape and a spiky beak-like top that made me think of herons and storks – but they resented having to pay when it first opened. Now admission is free. And its reputation has improved.

The weather had changed: we were back to Manchester drizzle, the fine rain like a sea fret, that swathes the city in mist. I arrived first at the conservatory café on the ground floor and settled in a window table furthest from the door where it would be possible to talk discreetly. Two other tables were occupied, a group of students clustered round one and a family of four who I thought were probably tourists (better dressed than most of us and sporting cameras) had the other.

Sipping my coffee, I looked out across the square, which is bounded by historic buildings. On the left was the Corn Exchange, the back of it. Four storeys high, perfect proportions, built in sandstone. On the right Urbis itself rose up, beyond it an old red-brick building with a pompous little turret on one end, Chetham's School of Music. And directly opposite I could see the medieval Manchester Cathedral with its square tower and tall vaulted windows and looming behind it the oblong of the Travelodge blurred in the rain.

At my side of the square on one of the lawned terraces, there was a large sculpture, sheets of metal bent and reminiscent of bows or wings or propeller blades, slightly menacing in its effect.

My stomach was tight with apprehension. I'd no idea what state Trisha would be in but she'd surely be upset if not angry at me. After all, I was the woman who had pointed the finger and cried murderer. As it was, she nodded politely when she arrived and bought a tea before joining me. She was impeccably turned out but her eyes were bloodshot and the frown line stayed etched deep between her eyes the whole time.

'I'm going away for a while.' She spoke very precisely and slowly as though there were a thousand words to choose from and she had to focus hard to pick the correct ones. 'Family in India.'

I wondered whether she was on tranquillisers. I nodded.

'He says it was an accident.' Her eyes filled instantly and she pressed a hand, a slender, beautifully manicured hand, to her mouth and blinked hard.

'You've seen Steve?'

'This morning. How could he?' Her face was alive with anguish. 'How could he do that to her? And now everything, our marriage, everything is a lie.'

'I'm sorry,' I told her.

'You don't have anything to be sorry for,' she said kindly. She ran her hands through her dark, choppy hair. 'I was so stupid. Janet was my friend, she was such a good friend and now – I can't even be angry with her because...I want to scream and shout at her and tell her what a...bitch she's been and find a way to sort it out but I can't do any of that.' Her face narrowed in anger. 'I feel like this,' she held thumb and finger an inch apart, 'this big. But so angry and I miss her. I miss him.' She pressed her hands to her cheeks and stared down.

Out of the corner of my eye I could see the tourists glancing our way; it would be hard to ignore the intensity coming from our table.

Trisha looked across at me. 'And Steve let me hire you. Do you think he wanted to be caught?'

'No. But you were very determined. He probably thought it would look odd if he tried to talk you out of it.'

'Will you give evidence?' she asked.

'Yes, if they want me to.'

'We never really know people, do we? The Mondays – he'd ask how my mum was. And I'd see Janet, the day after or the day after that. I never had a clue. It feels like the whole world knew, everyone but me.'

I shook my head. 'No one knew.' Janet and Steve had been great at keeping it secret.

'And then that day, he must have come home and been so normal. And in the days after he'd sit with me and listen to me worry about her, knowing—' She splayed her hands, fingers wide, waved them in a gesture – how crazy is that? 'And the children,' her voice broke, 'they've lost their mum and everything and I've thought about it but I just cannot deal with it now, with them. I think I'm cracking up. I just need to try and get through this. Does that sound selfish?'

'No. With the best will in the world, it's a horrendous situation. For all of you. Like you say, you need to find a way of coping. You have to think of yourself.'

'Mark probably wouldn't let me near them again, anyway.'

'It's not your fault, Trisha. None of it's your fault.'

'It doesn't feel like that,' she said through tears. She found a tissue in her bag, wiped her eyes. 'Thanks for seeing me. I just needed to explain to somebody before I left.'

'You're going soon?'

'Tomorrow.'

Sometimes running away is the right thing to do.

'Good luck,' I told her. 'And your mother?'

'She doesn't know me anymore. She spends half the evening asking me the same old questions, getting anxious, trying to work out who I am, who she is. I'll come back in a few months and we'll go through the whole palaver again. She won't know I've not been there.' She hesitated. 'There's one thing I wanted to ask you. A big favour, really. It's Hector.'

Aw, shit no, I thought; please don't ask me to take the dog. I'd acquired Digger by default in the course of a case and I could only cope with that because Ray took a shine to him and put himself in charge of all the dog-walking and feeding and so on.

'I've a friend who's going to have him while I'm away but she can't pick him up until the day after tomorrow.'

My heart eased.

'It'd just be twenty-four hours or so. I could bring him on my way to the airport and she'll collect him the next day.'

'Fine. No problem.' Twenty-four hours I could cope with and I was pleased I could help her out. Though Digger would probably take the hump.

Trisha dropped Hector off as arranged and we enjoyed a day of mayhem as Digger defended his territory from the bigger, more playful dog. There were periodic bouts of snarling and attempted savaging whenever anyone forgot to close the doors separating the dogs. A short-lived hassle.

My final invoice went in to the lawyer's office. And I put all my papers relating to the case in a file in case they called me as a witness. Though as it turned out they didn't need me.

CHAPTER THIRTY

When Steve Marlowe eventually gave evidence, his version of events wasn't far from my imaginings. Steve and Janet had been having an affair for over two years. Every Monday evening she would drive out to his house, knowing Trisha was out. On rare occasions they arranged to meet for lunch and took a hotel room, choosing places where they were unlikely to be recognised by anyone. But Janet began to chafe against the secrecy and talked about the two of them setting up home together. She knew she would lose her best friend as well as her husband but she was finding it harder than ever to live the lie. She and her children would have a bright future with Steve.

Steve was appalled. He'd no intention of leaving Trisha; he didn't want to be saddled with Janet and certainly not her children. He had a prosperous and unencumbered life. He wasn't about to throw it all away. He'd never promised Janet anything but he'd been happy to let her believe in her pipe dream. In early June, Janet presented him with a deadline. They must tell their respective spouses by the end of the summer. Around that time, she finished her last supply teaching post, bought new lingerie and cancelled her hair appointment.

At his trial, Steve Marlowe's barrister argued for manslaughter, denying that there had been any pre-meditation. I sat in court, watching Steve Marlowe as his lawyer led him through his defence. Marlowe was dressed in a dark-blue suit, a white shirt and a grey tie that matched the colour of his eyes. Like dirty ice. I wondered who'd picked that out. Was it in his wardrobe already? Or had someone bought it specially for his appearance? His gunmetal hair was still cut short and neat. He stood tall in the witness box, every inch a well-groomed, middle-class, professional man. His eyes slid over the people in the courtroom; when his gaze reached me I saw the sting of recognition there and a moment of intense dislike that disappeared as quickly as it had arrived.

'In your own words,' his barrister said, adjusting her gown 'take us through events once you reached Tarnghyll.'

'We parked at the edge of the quarry.' He spoke quietly but audibly. His face, with its weathered complexion, was sombre. 'I told Janet it was over.'

'You were in the car?'

'No, sorry.' He was quick to apologise. 'We got out; we were just near the car on the grass.'

'How did Janet react?'

Steve Marlowe was silent. He appeared to be struggling with his emotions, a gulping movement in his throat and muscles flickering along his jaw line. 'She—' He cleared his throat.

His nervousness was such a contrast to his manner in the days when his wife and I had been searching for Janet. Then he'd expressed some concern, comforted Trisha, shown an interest and chipped in with questions. The genial host who had made drinks and left us to it. Within earshot.

'She was hysterical. Screaming at me, crying and hitting me.'

'Were you surprised by this reaction?'

'Completely. I thought she'd be upset but she just went crazy.'

'What happened next?' his barrister asked.

'I tried to calm her down. I tried to get hold of her. She pulled away. She tripped and fell.'

The courtroom was almost silent, the relentless tick-tock of a wall clock measuring the suspense.

'She just lay there.' His voice fell to a whisper. 'She wouldn't get up. I tried to get her up. She wouldn't stand up.'

'And then?'

Steve Marlowe looked down at his hands. He was gripping the shelf of the witness stand. 'I panicked. She was dead.' He stopped abruptly. We all waited.

His barrister lifted her head. 'You didn't call for help?' she asked in a neutral tone.

'It was too late. I wasn't thinking straight. She wasn't breathing.' He covered his face with one hand.

The judge leant forward. 'Do you need a break, Mr Marlowe?'

'No.' He removed the hand and swallowed. His face was ashen now. 'I panicked. I couldn't bear to see her there, like that. I put her in the quarry.'

The prosecuting barrister, Mr Vaughan, was a dapper man with a slightly camp delivery. He picked away steadily at Steve Marlowe's account.

'You say Janet Florin became hysterical. What was she doing?'

'Crying, shouting, hitting me.'

'What was she shouting?'

'She was calling me a bastard, saying that I'd promised. That I couldn't do this to her.'

'Promised what, exactly?'

'To leave my wife for her.'

'Had you?' Mr Vaughan held his hands poised as if he'd clap at the right answer.

'Never.'

'Yet Mrs Florin had talked with you about a future together.'

'But I hadn't promised anything.'

'You led her to believe you would leave your wife.'

'No.' Marlowe frowned and shook his head.

'If you had never given her that understanding then on what basis did Janet Florin envisage a future with you?'

'I don't know.'

'In her distress did she threaten to tell your wife, to tell her husband about your relationship?'

'She might have done,' Marlowe said cautiously.

'Did she?'

'I think so.'

'And you had to ensure that didn't happen.' Mr Vaughan spoke quickly.

'No.' Marlowe looked around him as if seeking supporters.

'Did you love your wife?'

'Very much. I still do.'

'Is it true that her family are major shareholders in your company?'

There was a slight pause. Marlowe's barrister appealed to

the judge. 'Is this relevant, your honour?'

The judge raised his eyebrows at Mr Vaughan who nodded.

'Pertains to motive, your honour.'

'Proceed.'

Mr Vaughan turned on his heels and spoke to Marlowe. 'Trisha Marlowe's family are major shareholders in your company?'

'Yes.'

'If Janet Florin had told your wife about the affair, it might have signalled the end of your business as well as your marriage.'

'Not necessarily.' He sounded feeble. A false note that rang clearly round the room.

Mr Vaughan's face was a study in scepticism. He paused for effect then continued. 'I put it to you that you couldn't risk that. You fought with Janet Florin.'

'No. I tried to restrain her.'

'By cracking her head against a rock?'

An outburst of shocked laughter and murmurs of surprise greeted this brash description. The judge frowned.

'No,' Steve Marlowe said simply.

'Forensics have not been able to establish whether the blow to the head was caused by a fall or a blow. Did you pick up a rock and hit her with it?'

'No, she fell.'

Vaughan moved on. 'And seeing her there, injured. Did you administer CPR? Mouth-to-mouth resuscitation?'

The room grew very quiet again.

'No.'

'Did you feel for a pulse?'

'I can't remember.'

'Listen for a heartbeat?'

Steve Marlowe froze. His nose then his cheeks reddened.

'Mr Marlowe,' the prosecutor prompted.

'She was dead.'

'You've heard the post-mortem evidence, Mr Marlowe.'

'I thought she was dead,' Steve Marlowe insisted.

'Perhaps you hoped she was dead.'

'That's not true.'

'But to make absolutely sure, you throw her into deep water to drown.'

Another murmur swept through the court and Marlowe's barrister leapt to her feet. 'Objection, unnecessary badgering of my client.'

'Sustained,' snapped the judge.

'Withdrawn,' Mr Vaughan said immediately. 'Mr Marlowe, describe to the court, if you will, how you disposed of Mrs Florin's body.'

I had a sudden flash to the photo of Janet Florin; the one Trisha had given me where she was on holiday, smiling into the sun and showing the gap between her front teeth, her skin freckled and hair unruly.

While she took that last deadly walk with Steve Marlowe, her children were in school, her husband paying for sex in a deprived Liverpool suburb. None of them knowing that their world would come tumbling down before the day's end.

'I put it in the quarry,' Marlowe said.

'You were close to the car when you argued?'

'Yes.' He sounded a little puzzled.

'And she fell near that spot?'

'Yes.'

'So you had to move the body some considerable distance in order to reach the part of the crater where there was a clear drop? It would have taken a few minutes. Carrying her or dragging her. Yes?'

'I don't remember.'

'Why choose that location, Mr Marlowe? Miles from home, remote and isolated.'

Steve Marlowe cleared his throat. 'I knew it would be our last time together, Janet had never been there, it was private and—' He stalled.

'You are asking the court to believe you made a two-hour trip to break the news to your mistress that your affair was over. Knowing that you would have to travel back together for two hours?'

'Yes,' Marlowe said adamantly.

The jury weren't convinced; they returned a majority verdict of murder. Steve Marlowe is in prison in County Durham now.

Mark was able to clear his debts when Janet's insurance policy was settled. Eventually he'll get compensation from the criminal injuries board as well.

Trisha didn't attend the trial. I wasn't surprised. I wonder sometimes whether she came through it all intact. It must be hard for her to trust people, at the very least. It must be impossible for her to remember her friend without thinking of the betrayal. Janet Florin wasn't the only victim of Steve Marlowe's brutal actions.

* * *

Diane's operation was a success. She chose to have chemotherapy and did lose her hair and her eyebrows but, as she says, better bald than buried. It's growing back. She has a wicked line in outrageous wigs. Our friendship is more precious than ever. Each time we meet I rejoice that she's come through it so well. We've booked a holiday to Cuba, *Cuba!* early next year.

Ramin disappeared the day after he was discharged from hospital. One of the many failed asylum seekers determined to stay. He's probably working in some menial job, grieving for his brother, for his country and trying to keep safe. God, I wish him luck. I like to imagine he's come to terms with all he lived through and has fallen in love and found peace and is thinking of starting a family of his own. That maybe he still plays footie in some park every weekend and has learnt to smile again.

There is a photo on my office wall. Bob Swithinbank standing side by side with his birth mother Sandra. They're both beaming. Round cheeks, crinkled eyes. It came in the post one day. Made my heart swell.

Ray and I are in the kitchen. I'm doing the washing-up, he's sweeping the floor. He comes close, stands behind me and kisses my neck, making my muscles tighten, my skin tingle. I've been wondering whether to tell the kids that we're an item but there's no hurry. It's still so new.

Then a shriek pierces the air. 'Mummy, Mummy.' Maddie in the garden. Pulse spiking, I fly out. Digger gives a bark of alarm.

She's by the pond with Tom. 'Look!' She points. Excited not hurt. I catch my breath.

'Look, Dad,' Tom squeals, dances a little jig, 'a dinosaur.'

And it is. Tiny, tiny creature with lizard's paws, a delicate face, a frill round its neck, a slender tail. It's terracotta coloured, smooth and dull, with a line of colour along the edge. And for a moment I wonder if it's one of Tom's toys and they're winding me up. Then it swallows.

'It's a newt,' I say. 'Isn't it wonderful.'

Ray catches my eye, his look tender and a smile just showing. A thrill runs through me. I wonder how soon we can get the kids to sleep.